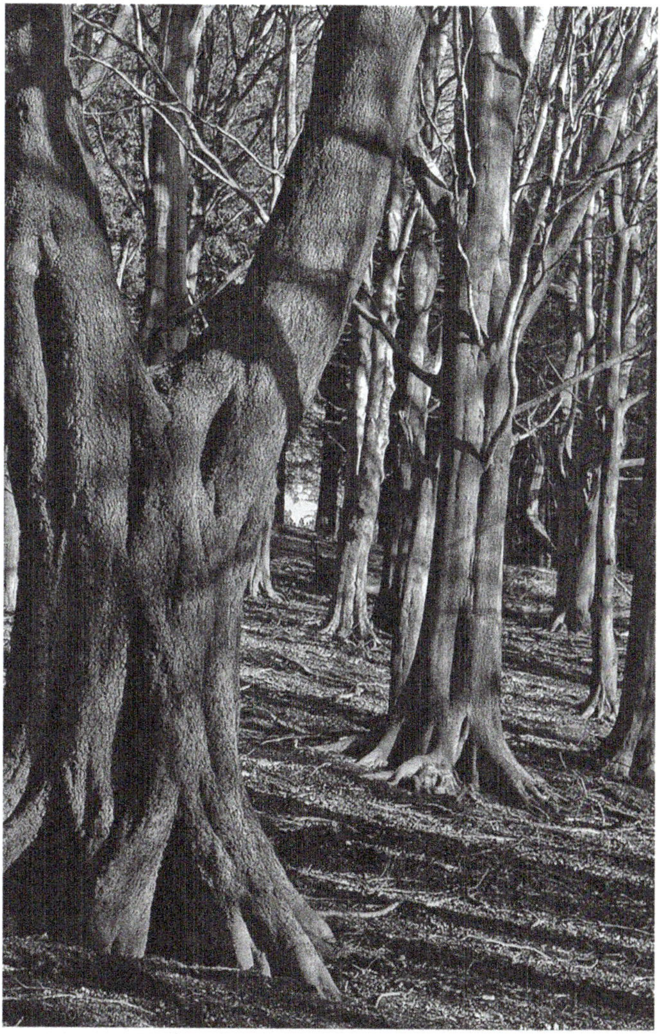

Willow Moon Publishing

https://willowmoonpub.com

Wind and Water: A Love Story
The Little Dragon Flies in the Sun
Nobody Reads Haiku
Granny Kat's The Frog Prince (play adaptation)
Granny Kat's Sleeping Beauty (play adaptation)
S.H Levan's Cookbook: Recipes from Victorian Lancaster County
Pepper, Ms. Pepperoni, Finds Someone to Love

Coming Soon:
Samuel Stanley Scotty Snight by Alison Broderick
Make a Wish on a Fish by Jennie Wiley
The Itch of Gloria Fitch: a play by Paul Hood
Sweet Treats Book of Cupcakes: A Love You a Brunch Cookbook edited by M. L. Ashly

Deadtime Stories

Kathryn Viers

Willow Moon Publishing

Lancaster, Pennsylvania

Willow Moon Publishing
Copyright © 2017 by Kathryn Viers
Published by Willow Moon Publishing
108 Saint Thomas Road
Lancaster, PA 17601
willowmoonpublishing.wordpress.com

Text © 2014 Kathryn Viers

All rights reserved. No part of this publication may be reproduced or transmitted in any form or by many means except for brief quotations in printed reviews, without the prior permission of the publisher.

Cataloging Data
Viers, Kathryn
Dead Time Stories/Kathryn Viers. –2nd U.S. Edition
Summary: A compilation of short stories based on aging, revenge, and the macabre.
Edited and Revised by Jennie Wiley
ISBN: 978-1-948256-02-5
Typeset: Cambria
Design by Jodi Stapler

This book is dedicated to all women who have triumphed over adversity and to my daughters; Jennifer, Jodi, and Jami.

Stories	Pages
NIGHTFALL	14
THE ULTIMATE REVENGE	26
I REALLY HATE MY JOB...	47
AND MOST OF MY COWORKERS!	47
A PLACE TO DIE FOR	61
THE BULLY	73
I'LL BE BACK FOR YOU	87
THE MASSACRE	103
SUNSHINE, SCALLOPS, AND SUICIDE	111
AN EVENING IN CHICAGO	121

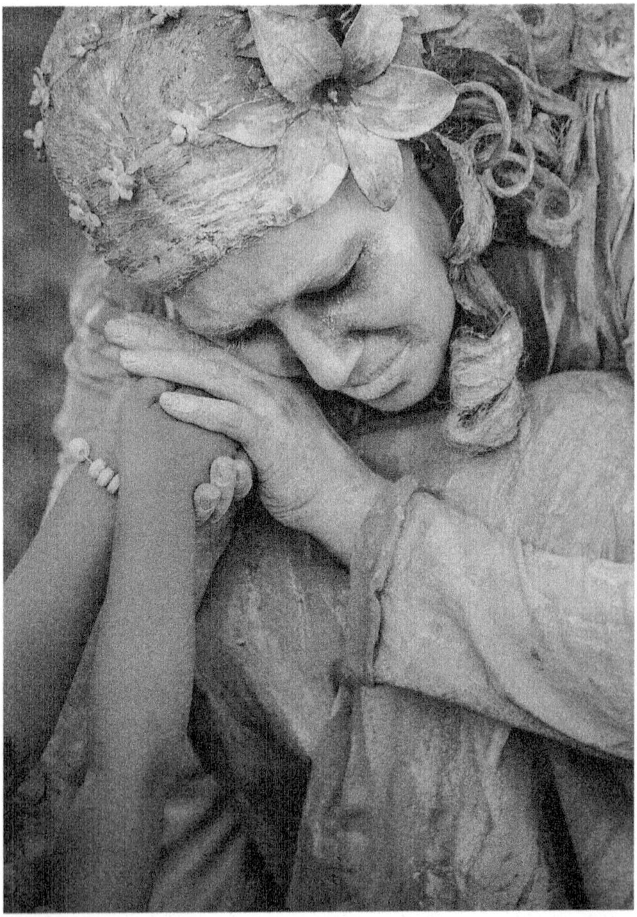

Nightfall

An eerie glow floated downward. It was not possible to tell from where, but as it reached the moss-covered ground, the light became a translucent sphere. Within the sphere lay a sleeping child, unclothed and approximately eight years of age.

Outside the sphere was a jungle. Ferns grew out of the mossy soil, fungi on the sides of the trees, and the air was filled with the clicks and whirs of insects. Night was falling as the sphere rested upon the earth. The child fluttered her eyes open, eyes too large for her heart-shaped face. She was pale as the moon and slender as the reeds. Sitting cross-legged in the sphere, the child placed her hands palm side outward and the luminous bubble exploded without a sound and the nude child
stepped onto the earthen floor, like a graceful cat.

At once there was silence. The breeze no longer whispered through the grasses and the insects were deafeningly quiet. Turning her back to the wooded area, the child walked in the direction of a small cottage at the edge of the trees. By the time the child had reached the door, to the small home; she had grown two inches and aged four years.

The cottage door opened before its residents knew she had arrived. An elderly woman stood in the door frame gazing lovingly at the small naked child.

"Oh, my dear, won't you come in and warm yourself by the fire. Houston, bring my robe and quickly!"

A gentleman matching her in age hustled to the woman carrying a burgundy and fleece bathrobe. She placed the robe on the child and led her to a rocking chair by their roaring fire. After the child was seated, the woman poured her a cup of hot tea and offered an introduction.

"My name is Dallas, and this is my brother, Houston. Yes, I know our names are a little silly." Dallas laughed, "Mother was from Texas and... well, there you have it then, don't you?"

The child considered Dallas' eyes and knew what was behind them, a kind and loving woman. A woman whose husband and child were lost many years ago and now cared for her bachelor brother with the love left from their departure. The siblings lived in the cottage for the past thirty years. Oh, they had their ups and downs, just like all brothers and sisters, but most of the time, they lived in tandem. Houston was engaged at one time, but diphtheria had wound its' way through the quaint village nearby, and taken Houston and Dallas' loved ones as a toll for its departure.

What Dallas saw as she considered the child's eyes, was knowledge, beauty, and a cagey reticence. Dallas could intuit easily and today she saw this young soul was troubled. She chose not to ask what the child was doing in the forest or why she was naked. Instead, she began with the basis.

"What is your name, dear?"

In a soft, silky voice, the child replied, "Giltrine."

The name sounded familiar to Houston and for the first time, he stole a long glance at the girl-child sitting in his rocking chair. The child looked as familiar as her name sounded.

"How old are you, Giltrine?" asked Houston, his eyes crinkled with age yet seeing her clearly for the first time since her arrival.

"At this moment, I am twelve."

"Houston, keep an eye on the child; I'll be back in a moment." Dallas hurried through a closed door while Houston openly stare at the familiar stranger. It seemed to Houston, he had seen that face before... and had loved it.

"Here, you can change into these, my dear," stated Dallas as she handed a pair of overalls and moccasins to Giltrine. "They are old and worn, but clean and mended since they last belonged to my daughter, Celeste. She was about your age when she died... along with my husband." Dallas' voice broke a tiny bit and she cleared her throat. "You can change in my bedroom," Dallas pointed to the door, she had just closed. Giltrine rose, gracefully, and carried the clothes into the bedroom.

Houston shook his head and then declared, "I have seen that child before! I know I have...and yet, how could it be?"

"I know, Houston, I know. She does look like someone we've known. I just can't seem to remember, who," His sister answered,

"Maybe we should take care offering her a place to rest for the night, Dallas."

"Oh, hush, Houston! She's perfectly harmless! Why, she's just a mere girl, like my Celeste was."

17

As Houston opened his mouth to reply, Giltrine walked back into the room, handed Dallas the robe, and sat back down in the old rocking chair. "Giltrine, suppose you stay the night and then tomorrow we'll try to find your family?"

"I don't have a family." She said in the same soft voice, "May I not stay with you and Houston for a little while?"

"I don't know if that's possible. Is that possible, Dallas?" Houston interrupted.

"Of course, it's possible, you old fool," his sister snapped, "Giltrine may stay here as long as she likes. You can sleep in the loft in that little daybed." She turned toward the child, "The room is clean, and you can see the forest from the window."

"That's sounds wonderful, Dallas," Giltrine' turned to face Houston, "Houston, are you troubled by me?"

"No, he's not troubled by anything, unless it's not having his supper by now. I'll get it on the table right away," Dallas hastened into the kitchen, but gave Houston a very nasty look as she went by him.

"No, I'm not troubled. I just seem to think I might have seen you somewhere; before. You from around here," Houston asked.

"No, I'm from around...well, everywhere."
"Folks travel a lot, then?"

"I have no folks, Houston; but yes, I travel a lot."

"How does a young sprig of a girl, like you, get around without clothing; seeing that you're sitting there with my niece's belongings on your back," Houston leaned in.

Giltrine uncrossed her fingers, which she had place behind her back, and gave Houston a smile that could melt any old coot into a stuttering fool, "I fell in the river and my clothing was very wet and cold. I always heard that wet and cold clothing can be worse for a person's health than bare skin. I left them by the river and the path brought me to you."

That smile played its trick. Houston was eating out of the palm of Giltrine's hand. "Well that makes sense to me. I always heard that tale, too. Dallas? Supper ready? Giltrine and I are mighty hungry," Houston turned to Giltrine and smiled in return. He realized that the girl seemed to belong in this house with Dallas. Or, maybe with him. He only knew he was beginning to become very comfortable with her company.

"But, you hardly ate a thing. You need to keep up your strength, if you're going to get over this, dear," Dallas reprimanded.

"You hardly ate a thing. You need to keep up your strength, if you're going to get over this, dear."

"Get over what, Dallas?"

"Why, diphtheria," Dallas answered."

"Dallas, I don't have diphtheria, that was your daughter, Celeste; wasn't it? I'm Giltrine," she answered.

"Of course, you're not Celeste. I don't know why I said that. At first when Celeste became ill I could get her to eat, but as the illness progressed, she didn't want food. She was so hot, and I'd have to bathe her in cool water and then I'd have to change her clothing and sheets. After a while it was just better to leave the child nude, under the cool fresh sheets. I just got confused," Dallas offered in explanation.

"How terrible to lose a child and a husband," The girl said looking at her hands.

Dallas' voice grew fainter as she replied, "Yes, it was terrible. I wanted to die too, but Houston needed me. He lost someone also." Houston very rarely spoke of that period in his life and never to a stranger, but for some reason he wanted to unburden himself of the memories to Giltrine.

20

"Yes, I lost my fiancé, Julia. We were to be married the following month, but she was taken so fast, I couldn't even arrange for the traveling minister to come any earlier. I wanted her to know that I loved her and wanted her as my wife no matter what, but there wasn't any time," Houston remembered her with care. "She was beautiful with long wavy brown hair and big blue eyes…and graceful…she walked as if she floated. She was smart and funny. Isn't it strange that she'd fall for a country bumpkin, like me?"

"But she did, Houston. Love sees nothing but beauty," Houston turned his head toward Giltrine, "that is exactly what Julia would have said! Funny- you look a lot like Julia," Houston's voice grew quiet.

"I think she looks like my Celeste; same hair, same age, same way of talking- like a song" Dallas responded.

Houston nodded his head, "You're right, Dallas, she does remind me of Celeste, but at the same time I see Julia in her too."

"Dallas, Houston…would you like to see Julia and Celeste?" Giltrine rose from the chair and placed a small cold hand on the shoulders of the brother and sister. Houston and Dallas felt as if an electric wire had been placed upon them and they looked in fright at one another. "You don't have to be afraid; not of me. Dallas, you know who I am and what I came for."

The pain was no more, and Dallas and Houston began to feel tired but peaceful, like you do after shoveling snow all morning and then relaxing with a hot chocolate. Giltrine led Houston to his rocking chair, by the fire, and bent to kiss him on the cheek. "Goodnight, Houston. Julia is waiting," she whispered. Taking Dallas' hand, Giltrine guided the elderly woman to her seat by the large sewing table. Dallas was gently pushed into her seat and once again, Giltrine brushed a soft kiss on Dallas' forehead. "Goodnight, sweet Dallas. Celeste and Thomas are waiting for you."

Houston's and Dallas' eyelids grew heavy and slowly closed... as a smile appeared on each wrinkled, but contented face. "Goodnight to you dear brother and sister. You had a long life; both bitter and sweet, but now it is nightfall and your loved ones await you on the other side." Dallas and Houston each inhaled deeply and then their chests grew still, their breathing silent.

The translucent sphere reappeared within the cottage and surrounded Giltrine. It floated up and out through the window, and the child inside began to grow younger, until she was just a tot ...an infant...a newborn...the nothing. The light faded, and the night was once again- its darkened and peaceful self.

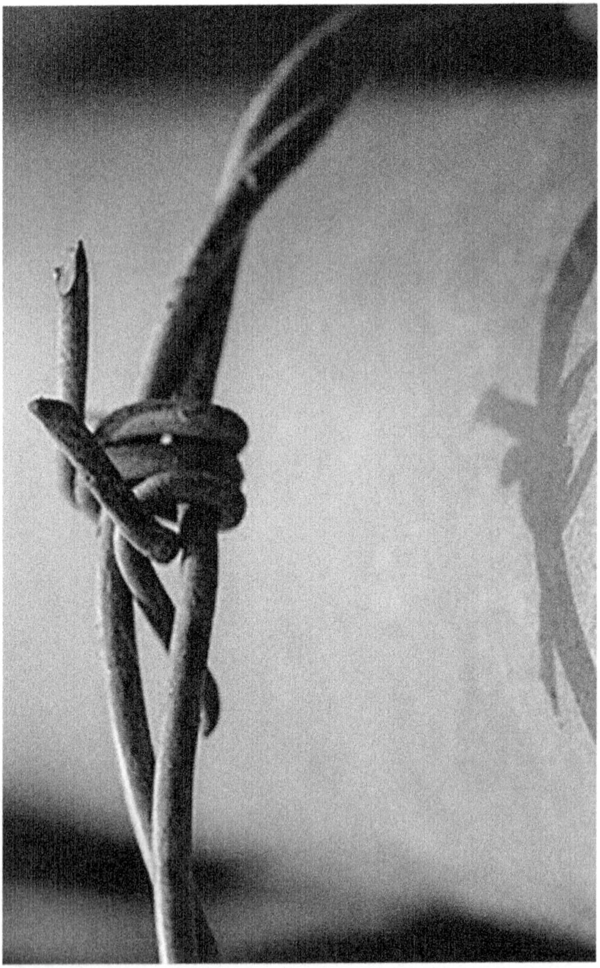

The Ultimate Revenge

The day she found out her body was dying, she also found out that her emotional body was already dead. Coming home from the doctor's office with grave news about the lump, she wanted the comfort and loving arms of her husband around her. What she got was a scene right out of a movie she had witnessed a long time ago.

She guessed he didn't hear the door or her call. She guessed he didn't hear the stairs, where there was always a creak when someone stepped on them. He was much too busy having sex with his secretary... on her bed. As if she was completely frozen in place by what she was seeing, she could not move. Suddenly, the mistress opened her lust-
filled eyes and gazed across the room. The tramp's smile grew smug as she whispered into the man's ear, "I love you!"

He replied, fiercely, as he made love, "Oh, my god, I love you, too!"

"Are you going to tell her, today? Are you going to leave that bitch, today?"

"Yes, yes! I don't love her anymore, I love you! I want you!"

"Good! I haven't been able to cope with you going home every night to her. I've already left my husband and now, today, is the day for you!" Both sighed and then the bed was still.

He turned over on his back and glanced toward the open doorway. Seeing her standing there, he quickly tried to cover his naked body with the sheet, while the temptress lay flaunting her almost perfect shape not caring who saw her. She smiled at the wife's tear-filled eyes and laughed as the woman turned quickly around and left the room. He heard the creak on the steps and the front door open...then close.

That was the last time she would be seen by him for quite a while.

The plan came into her mind so fast, it was almost as if someone were telling her what to do. She knew this would take some time to set up and yet, she had at least three months; that should be plenty of time to set this plan into motion. First, she had to locate a certain, Andrew Carboni and talk things over with him. This was going to work! It just had to!

That evening, she mulled over the details in her mind. Nothing could be written down, nothing said to any person, with the exception of one, and he wouldn't talk if he valued his freedom.

The phone rang as she lay on the hotel bed, causing her to jump. She picked up the receiver and Andrew's voice came back at her from the other end. They spoke for over an hour. She questioned him about his location. His answer was just what she wanted to hear. She asked him when it would take place. His answer pleased her. She questioned whether he would be able to acquire all of the needed materials to get the job done. His answer calmed her. They hung up.

The next day, she sent off a letter to her insurance agent with her new policy's rate increase and signatures at the bottom. She called her attorney and filled in some missing pieces he needed to know. It was all accomplished with a dramatic and tragic tone. The attorney understood her meaning and made her a promise. She smiled to no one. So far, the plan was working to a "T".

She wrote two notes, addressed each and drove to a neighboring town to drop them off in the mailbox, outside of the mistress' apartment. She saw his truck. He was there! She began to cry silent tears, and it was difficult to drive back to the hotel. Once in her room, she lay down on the bed and flipped on the television and watched Survivor.

A month later, she was lying on a cold metal gurney with a bullet hole in the back of her head. The insurance company needed to have an autopsy performed in order to conclude if her death was a suicide or homicide.

Two weeks later, the police handcuffed the mistress and took her into the station, while plain clothed detectives watched her husband for signs of guilt. They followed him from his mistress' apartment to the jail and back again. The detectives were waiting for the autopsy results and the weapon of choice.

They found two weapons. One was in the tramp's apartment and the other in an old junked car that was waiting to be crushed. An anonymous tip led them to the junkyard. They finally had enough evidence to take to the District Attorney and to make a second arrest. The husband and his mistress were both booked on murder in the first degree.

Of course, the defendants vehemently denied the charges, claiming there was no evidence, no proof, no reason! The cops had heard all of that before.

With a plea of Not Guilty, the prosecution and the defense prepared for the court date and thankfully, the husband and mistress did not need to wait very long.

The community was in an outrage and wanted someone's blood, so the trial was pushed forward on the judge's docket.

The Prosecutor planned on calling eight witnesses to the stand, the defense; only two. "All rise! This court is now in session." The judge rapped on his desk with the polished wooden gavel, "Gentlemen, you're opening statements, please."

The Prosecutor rose and addressed the jury, "Ladies and gentlemen of the jury, the prosecution will prove beyond a reasonable doubt that this man and this woman conspired and carried out the murder of this man's wife. We will prove - that not only did they try one method to end his wife's life, but used another, more swift method of disposal. At the end of this trial, you must find both defendants guilty of murder in the first degree and if that is the case, the State will seek the Death Penalty." The Prosecutor took his seat.

The defense attorney rose, and he too addressed the jury, "Ladies and gentlemen, by the time you have heard all of the "so called" evidence and have listened to my clients, you will know that the verdict should be Not Guilty!" The defense attorney took his seat.

The prosecutor called is first witness, "I call the coroner to the stand."

"What were the findings of the autopsy, as far as the homicide was concerned... only the homicide."

"We found a large amount of rat poison in her blood and stomach and a gunshot to the head."

"Which method actually killed the deceased?"

"Both resulted in her death. The rat poison was placed in her diet coke and as she lay near death from the poison, she was shot. Both or either one killed, or could have killed, the deceased."

"Your witness."

"No questions," said the defense attorney.

"Call your next witness."

"The State calls the Allstate Insurance Agent."

He was sworn in and then asked, "Did the deceased and her husband have any life insurance policies?"

"Yes, they both did."

"What was the amount of each policy?"

"The Mister had a one-hundred-thousand-dollar policy and so did the Mrs. However, the Mister had added another four-hundred thousand dollars onto her policy. I received the signed policy and the rate increase, in the mail."

"Who signed the policy and the check?"

"The policy was signed by the Mister and an unknown person. The check was only signed by the Mister."

"Thank you. No more questions."

"Your witness," the prosecutor ceded.

"How do you know that the policy and the check had actually been written by the husband?" he asked.

"We didn't know for sure, but then we took the signatures from past policies and this new one to a handwriting expert and he corroborated that the signature on both the policy and the check had been written by the same person who had signed previous policies. He did not make a match with the Mrs.' signature. That is why I know it was signed by another person. The Mister had inquired as to the policy a couple of days after the deceased was murdered. That is when we became suspicious and examined the policies a lot closer."

"No more questions, your Honor."

"I now call, Detective Bob to the stand."

"Detective, could you please describe the manner in which, you believe, or know, the deceased met her final rest?"

"Yes. We believe that the female defendant went to the deceased's hotel while the deceased was out, placed rat poison in the deceased's diet coke which was sitting on the night stand, and left. Approximately, ten minutes later, the husband entered the hotel room, stayed for a short time, left, and then returned fifteen minutes after that. The deceased was shot through the mouth and the gun placed in her right hand, as if to indicate a suicide."

"How do you know both defendants were at that particular hotel, on that particular night?"

"We have surveillance video of both defendants arriving at separate times and entering the hotel. Some of the hotel's staff identified the husband as entering the room and leaving in a rush. We have the female defendant's fingerprints all over the coke bottle and found a can of rat poison in her apartment. Even though the gun had the deceased's fingerprints, it also contained her husband's. We found out that the defendants were having an affair and that the deceased caught them in bed together. We also know that there was a threat against the deceased's life. You have already heard of an increase in life insurance benefits, which were made out
to the hubby; as sole beneficiary. This case was a slam dunk!"

"You witness," the prosecutor nodded toward the defense.

"No questions, your Honor."

"I would like to call Attorney Joe to the stand."

"Attorney Joe, you were the deceased's divorce lawyer, were you not?"

"Yes, I was."

"Did the deceased ever tell you anything in confidence about being afraid for her life?"

"Yes. Two weeks before she was murdered, I received a phone call. She explained to me that the female defendant threatened to "get rid" of her. The defendant ranted that she would make sure the Mrs. never spoke to the husband again. Whether it was by knife, gun, or poison, the defendant was going to be rid of the problem once and for all. The deceased wanted me to know what had happened, just in case, there was a tragic ending."

"The State rests for now, your Honor, but we would like to reserve one more witness until after the defense has ended with his witnesses."

"The defense may call its first witness."

"I call the husband of the deceased to the stand."

The husband slowly took his seat and was sworn in. He swore to tell the truth, the whole truth, and nothing but the truth, so help him God; the only problem with that statement was that the husband did not believe in God.

"Sir, could you please tell me… have you ever signed an insurance policy to increase your wife's benefits?"

"No, sir, I didn't."

"Did you purchase a handgun and take that gun to your wife's hotel and shoot her?"

"No, sir, I didn't."

"Have you signed anything in the past two months that was connected to your marriage?"

"Yes sir. I signed divorce papers, that night in my wife's hotel room. She sent me a note stating that her lawyer needed the papers the next day, and I needed to sign them that very night. That's why I was there. I went to her room, signed the papers, and left. I did not return!"

"Did you inquire about your wife's insurance policy after she was murdered?"

"Yes sir. I needed to bury her, didn't I? I didn't have the money for the coffin and stuff. Isn't that the reason someone buys life insurance, in the first place?"

"No further questions, your Honor."

"Your witness."

"Thank you, your Honor. Isn't it true you have been having an affair with the female defendant-your secretary- for the past six months?"

"Yes, that's true. But, I wasn't ever going to leave my wife! The only reason we were separated was because she came home unexpectedly and caught us in bed! I would never have left my wife for ...her!"

"Did you kill your wife?"

"No, I did not!"

"Do you know how your fingerprints got on the gun?"

"No, I do not!"

"Do you know anyone who might have wanted to see your wife dead?"

"Yes!"

"Who might that be, sir?"

The husband jumped off his chair and pointed directly to his codefendant and yelled, "She did! If anyone murdered my wife, it was her!"

"Sit down, sir!"

"Are you trying to make us believe, that your mistress would have more to gain from this murder than you would?"

"That's exactly what I'm saying!"

"Do you know how the gun got into that old T-bird you had junked?"

"No, I don't. I took a lie detector test! Doesn't that hold any weight?"

"It might, sir...if you had passed. No more questions, your Honor."

"I would like to call my female defendant to the stand," the defense attorney said.

"Were you having an affair with the deceased's husband?"

"Yes, and he did love me too. He was going to leave his wife. He's lying if he says he wasn't! I had nothing to do with her death. I don't know how that poison got into my apartment or how my fingerprints got on that coke bottle! I just know- I didn't do it!"

"Thank you. No further questions."

"Your witness."

"Did you threaten the deceased?"

"No!"

"You were shown at the hotel in question on the surveillance cameras. Now, if you weren't there to hurt anyone, why were you there?"

"I received a letter stating I had won a free weekend at that hotel and spa. I had to go to the hotel to collect the voucher."

"Did you receive the voucher? Could you show us the voucher?"

"I don't have it. It was to be mailed to me and I wasn't at home to get my mail; if you get my meaning."

"No voucher! You also did not pass the lie detector test and your fingerprints were at the murder scene. What a coincidence."

"I didn't even know his wife was staying at that hotel!"

"No more questions to this witness, your Honor."

"The witness may step down. Do you have any other witnesses, Mr. Defense?"

"No, the defense rests."
"Mr. Prosecutor?"

"Yes, your Honor. I would like to call, the deceased's oncologist to the stand."

A well-dressed middle-aged man took his seat and took the oath of honesty.

"Doctor, you were the deceased's physician?"

"One of them, yes."

"What were you treating her for?"

"Cancer. She had cancer."

"What all was involved with this cancer?"

"It was affecting her glands, liver, and brain. A month before she was killed, I had given her three months or less to live. She was very upset and wanted only to go home and talk to her husband. I imagine that was the day she caught him in bed with another woman and she never had a chance to tell him."

"Thank you, doctor. I have neither more questions nor witnesses. I have no closing statement, except to say, considering all the testimony you have heard, you can only vote to convict and for those two monsters to receive either the death sentence or life without parole. The Prosecution rests."

"Does the Defense wish to state any closing arguments?"

"The Defense rests your honor."

"The jury may be excused to deliberate, and this courtroom is on standby."

The judge rapped his gavel, the jury filed out the back, and the courtroom emptied.

As the spectators filed into the atrium, the insurance agent spied Mr. Andrew Carboni and hurried after him. "Excuse me, Mr. Carboni, isn't it?"

"Yes, may I help you?"

"Yes. I'm the deceased's insurance agent and two days before she was killed she called and transferred her benefits to her best friend, Andrew Carboni. Here is your check, sir. She was a lovely woman, and I bet an even lovelier friend."

Carboni took the envelope and with his head down, sobbed for affect and stated quite seriously, "She was a wonderful friend and person. I met her years ago when we happened to work at the same school. I loved her very much."

Turning away, they heard the bailiff call. "The jury has reached a verdict. All spectators wishing to be in the court room, must enter now!"

The room began to swell with people, like a sponge fills with water. All were seated. The lawyers and the defendants entered and then took their places. Finally, the judge and the twelve jury members took their places.

"Ladies and gentlemen of the jury have you reached a verdict?"

"We have, your Honor."

"Bailiff, please pass me the verdict."

A paper was passed from the jury captain to the bailiff to the judge. The judge read the note, passed it back to the bailiff, and the bailiff passed it back to the jury captain.

"What say the jury?"

"We find the defendants GUILTY of murder in the first degree and recommend Life Imprisonment without parole.

"Do you all agree with this verdict?"

The jury spoke in unison, "We do- your honor."

"Will the defendants please rise." They did.

"You have been found guilty of murder in the first degree and have been preliminarily sentenced to life without parole. I shall grant this sentence, but before this court is adjourned, I would like to add. Both of you are the most heinous of monsters. Not only did you take the life of a human being, but you couldn't wait for three months for that poor woman to die. I hope that every day of your incarceration, you both will remember the deceased and the penalty for being a dark- hearted soul. Take them away! Court is adjourned."

As the courtroom cleared, only two people in the whole world knew exactly who killed the deceased. One was the deceased, who would no longer be tempted to brag about her ultimate revenge and the other, Mr. Andrew Carboni, just blew a kiss toward Heaven and mouthed the words, "Thank you" as he strutted out of the courthouse, fanning himself with a five-hundred-thousand-dollar check.

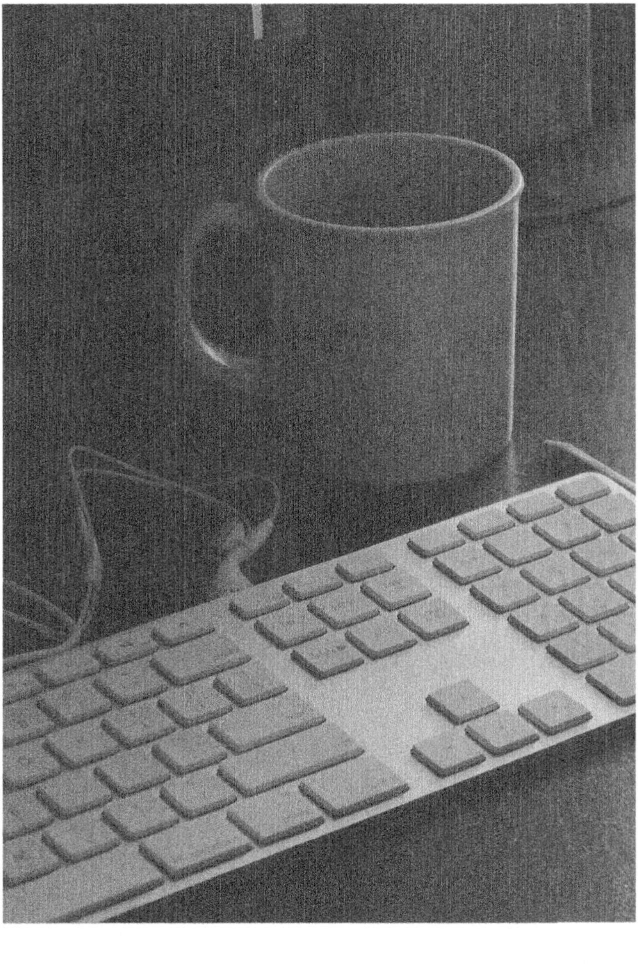

I Really Hate My Job...
and Most of My Coworkers!

I work in a large corporate office. I work for a worldwide corporation called, Hico Tectonics. Our offices are, get this, situated on Fooling Hell Road. Isn't that a trip? I don't think Hico is fooling hell at all. The place is Hell! I really hate my job and most of my coworkers. Those people annoy the shit out of me, with the exception of one or two. Most are driving me crazy.

"Finally," I thought, when I opened my apartment door, "I'm away from that Hell-hole." I was totally exhausted and just wanted to go to sleep. I had worked a couple of extra hour's overtime tonight, and I was beat but really needed a shower. I felt sticky and sweaty. After showering and grabbing a cup of coffee, I fell into bed and immediately to sleep.

The alarm clock's buzzing sound ricocheted through my body. I slammed my palm on the off button, as if the clock had done this on purpose to me. Another day at Hico. I really hated my job! I crawled out of bed and began my monotonous, normal routine; that is until I reached my destination...Hico. Police cars and an ambulance filled the back-parking spaces. Damn, I thought, now I have to walk clear around from the front! Who the hell got sick and caused the parking lot to be blocked? I really hate people!

By the time I reached my floor, I was pissed off and when I turned the corner to my office area and there was yellow crime scene tape across the entrance. Looking around, I spied my boss, MT, and strolled over to him to ask the most pertinent question of the day,

"What's going on and will we get paid for this?"

MT turned to me and in disgust and replied, "We better get paid for this, especially since it's not my fault someone was murdered last night!"

"Who was murdered?"

"Chatty Cathy. Gina found her this morning with her face full of staples and her mouth stapled shut. There was a note attached to her chin."

Trying desperately not to laugh in the face of tragedy, I asked, "What did the note say?"
MT leaned close to me and opened his mouth to answer. Whoa, that man's breath reeked!
Holding my breath, as best as I could, I heard him say, the note said…'finally, you've shut up'!"

That's when I lost it! I could no longer hold back the laughter, and it burst out of my mouth like a huge bubble popping; big and loud!
Seeing me in stitches must have hit MT's funny bone, because he began to go into laugh hysterically as he said, "It is funny, isn't it? She was a talker!" I couldn't speak and just nodded.

Evidently, no one else thought it funny, especially the police, who immediately gave us the "devil" eye. Uh-oh, now we were going to be suspects and for some unknown reason, that thought started me on another laughing journey, which was followed by MT's chicken cackle and made the police glare at us even more!

The police finally cleared our area so we could go back to work…oh, joy! Before I had a chance to place my butt into my half-broken chair, I was being guided by the elbow into MT's office. Oh, great! I bet I won't get paid for this!

"Miss Harnish, is it?"

"Yes, that's me."

"What did you think of the deceased, Cathy Myers?"

"Not much. I try not to think about my coworkers very much. It only brings me down, but Cathy was annoying and such a talker. That's all she did, no work, just talk!"

Oops, now I'd done it. Once again, I was too honest. I am in big, and I mean BIG, trouble!

"What time did you leave work, last evening, Miss Harnish?"

"I worked two hours over time- so I guess it was about seven. You can check my time card, if you'd like."

"We already did, you clocked out at seven, but did you leave at seven? Was there anyone in the office when you left?"

"It took me a little bit to get to my car, but I suppose I left the parking lot at seven-ten, seven-fifteen. MT, Janice, Portia, and Cathy were all still here when I left."

"Thank you, Miss Harnish. You may go back to work."

I stood up to leave and then turned back around and asked, "Do you know if we're going to get paid for this?"

"To be honest, Miss Harnish, I have my doubts."

"Damn! That's what I thought!"

I went back to my shared cubicle where a stack of papers lay in front of my computer. I turned to my desk partner and nastily inquired, "Couldn't you have stapled these papers, instead of just shoving them on my desk?"

"I tried to staple them, but your stapler is empty."

"Oh, sorry, I'll refill it."

After the police had questioned MT, Janice, and Portia, they packed up their forensic kits and left. A memo came through on the computer, telling me I had to make up today's lost time.

Great! Something beyond our control and we have to make up the time. Well, I guess I'll stay late tonight and get it over with.

Almost everyone had left by five and I still had two hours to make up. By the time I left, only MT, Portia, Janice, and some new guy, who I didn't know and didn't care to know, were still working or making out like they were working. I flipped off my computer screen and headed for home.

Once in my apartment, I grabbed my Triscuits, hurried through a shower to get the pencil smudges off my fingers, and settled down to watch Deadliest Catch. I don't even remember what that show was about. I fell asleep before the first commercial and was once again jolted awake by that damned infernal alarm clock. This morning, I did pick it up and throw it across the room. There! That'll teach it to wake me up!

All the way to work, I just kept saying over and over, "I really hate my job! I really hate my job!" I really did, you know.

I was stopped by a police cruiser, as I tried to turn into the parking lot of Hico. What now?

A policeman approached my car and I pushed the button to roll the window down- just a crack. "Yes, officer, what is happening today, at dear old Hico Tectonics?"

"Do you work here, miss? "

"Yes, I do."

"Could I have your name please?"

"Miss J. Harnish."

The cop looked over a clipboard filled with names, found mine and checked it off the list.

"You're free to go in, Miss Harnish, but use the front entrance. Oh, and Detective Carl wants to have a word with you. He's waiting in your office area. Have a good day."

"Yeah, you too." I mumbled. What now?

Again, as it was yesterday, we were not allowed into our office area. But this time instead of learning any or all information from MT, I was assaulted by the police detective and quickly led into an empty office.

"Miss Harnish, what time did you leave your office last evening?"

"The same time I left the night before; seven. Check the time card. I pulled out of the parking lot around seven-ten or seven fifteen. Janice, MT, Portia, and a new guy...don't know his name...were the only ones left in the office, when I left. I went straight home, did not pass go, and did not collect one-hundred dollars. I took a shower, got into my pajamas, ate some crackers, and started to watch Deadliest Catch until I fell asleep. Does that answer all your questions?"

"I think so... for now."

"Could you please tell me what is going on around here and am I going to get paid for today, at least?"

"I have no clue about the pay, but this MT fellow...he's dead. He was used as a human dartboard, but instead of darts, the killer used very sharp number four, pencils."

"Oh... my... God! Who's going to sign my overtime papers? Just kidding! What's happening, here? This place was a hell-hole before, but now it's a death trap too."

"MT was not the only victim, Miss Harnish. That Portia lady, she was bitten by an animal and bled to death in the parking lot. We think it could have been a brood of bull dogs."

"Well, then, there you go. It had to be Janice or that new guy!"

"I hate to disappoint you, but Janice and that new guy are also, both, very DEAD!"

"No, they can't be. What happened to them? A paper cut?"

"Strange that you should refer to paper, Miss Harnish. It seems that Janice was trimmed in the paper cutter."

"Wait a minute! I was just kidding! What happened to the new guy?"

"The new guys name was, Joe, and he was sent to shipping, bubble wrapped and all. It seems that you were the last person to see any of the victims, Miss Harnish."

"Other than the person who killed them you mean, because I had nothing to do with these murders!"

"Your stapler was empty yesterday. Your tape dispenser is missing today, and there is a large empty box, inside your cubicle, stamped with Lead Pencils/#4. A coincidence? I think not, Miss Harnish!"

"I didn't do anything!"

"Do you like your job...your coworkers...Miss Harnish?"

"I really do hate my job...and most of my coworkers; but I didn't do it! I didn't do it!"

"You're under arrest for murder, Miss Harnish."

I screamed as he handcuffed me, "I didn't murder anyone! Please, I didn't do it...I didn't do it!"

I heard a familiar buzz. That damn alarm clock. How dare it wake me up! Wait a minute! I'm in my bed. I'm waking up! It was only a dream. Thank you, God! I jumped out of bed, and before you knew it, I was on my way to that glorious place, Hico Tectonics. I love that place! Freedom is such an underrated feeling!

I was still ecstatic as I hit the parking lot - no cops...still grinning from ear to ear as I went into the office area - no yellow crime tape...still smiling as I proceeded to my cubicle - my tape dispenser was filled and on my desk...then I saw MT!

"You're two minutes late. You'll have to make up the time at lunch."

As that bum turned around to walk away, I picked up a very sharp, number four pencil and aimed. It hit his head, eraser side up. MT turned around and I quickly won an Oscar for my, it wasn't me, look.

Janice and Portia were working...but not working, and Cathy was talking a mile-a-minute. Well, it's the same old same old.

You know what I just realized? I really *do* hate my job...*and* most of my coworkers!

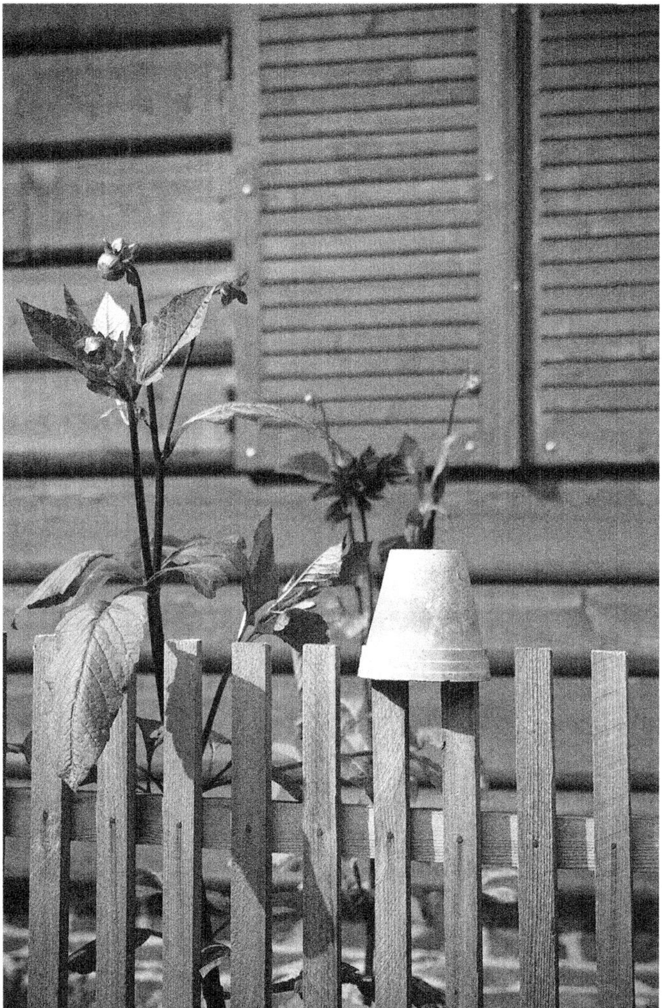

A Place to Die For

It was her sixtieth birthday and she woke up with a feeling of sadness and dread. Today, she will have to say goodbye to all of her loved ones. Today, her daughter, her grandchildren, her best friend, she must leave them all behind...it was the law!

They say the earth is running out of room. Between medical breakthroughs and increased health consciousness, death doesn't come as early these days. Sixty is considered disposable and a good age to make room for the new ones being born. Earth's population prompted the Global United Council's global law that upon your sixtieth birthday, you would be "retired". No one knew exactly what that meant, but, it happened all the same. At first, the world leaders had rejected the plan and the law did not pass for a few years, but with the continual growing population, and diminishing natural resources, the law was finally agreed upon.

The last law passed by the GUC took aim at procreation. for each married couple, there could be only one child. If that couple divorced and remarried, the new couple was permitted another child, but that only worked for the first divorce and remarriage. Everyone accepted the laws with less protest than you would expect. Our species suffers from a short view of the future.

A birthday party was planned for her, today and all her friends and family would attend. There would be happy stories and many hugs and kisses would be exchanged. As the day grows to an end, a bus would come for her and she will board with only one bag of belongings; she was to give her other personal items to the friend or family member of her choice. Inside the bus will be other sixty-year-old men and women-all going to the same place for *retirement...*

She didn't feel like getting out of bed, nor did she feel like attending her *going away* celebration. Her daughter was sad, at her leaving, but had encouraged her to pack her bag and to distribute her belongings weeks before.

Her daughter explained that it would be "much less of a stressful time for you...and for all of us", she had added quickly, which hadn't made her feel more cheerful. She stretched and the familiar cramps in her legs welcomed her to the morning.

Hopping out of bed, she hobbled around the room to warm up her muscles and coax the leg pain into submission. Once the cramps subsided she realized there was no use in going back to sleep. Her daughter was picking her up very soon; much too soon, for her liking.

After showering and dressing, she carried her suitcase into the living room, one of her favorite rooms in the house. It was so light and airy, and she would miss it.
She gazed at her suitcase and tried to remember what she had packed. Oh, yes! Six changes of casual clothing, four nighties, a good dress, her sensible pumps, extra sneakers, and a pair of slippers. A picture of her late husband, who had died of natural causes, two years before the *retirement* law was put into effect, and a picture of her daughter and her grandson and granddaughter, tucked in with her things. Toiletries were stuffed in the front pockets, and of course her medicines, it wasn't much to show for a lifetime of work and living.

Her home would be turned over to the State, her special belongings she had left to her daughter and her books to her grandchildren; except for her collection of Dickens and Austin. She had taken them to the library and had them copy all the chapters and words onto a small disc, which she could play anytime on her reader which she had also placed amidst her clothing.

Hearing a vehicle enter her drive, brought her to the present. Peeking out around the corner of the drapery, she had an impulse to run out the back door and hide.

"Yoo-hoo, mom, are you ready?"

It was too late to run so she picked up her suitcase and walked with her daughter to her transport. She never could call these things cars, they were much too small and way too slow. Opening the door, she crawled in and sat in the small passenger seat. Before she had time to sing the "Star Spangled Banner", it seemed they had reached Celebration Hall. There was a large sign on the front lawn that read, "Happy Sixtieth Birthday! Have a Great Retirement. We will miss you. Love..." and then all of her family and friends had placed their signatures all over the paper.

She wondered what they were referring to when they wrote the word, "retirement". How would they to know if that's what was happening. No one ever spoke about where they were sent, and no one ever received news from the "over-sixty" crowd, once they left. Although, they all promised to send postcards and write, no one ever did. Those left behind, didn't seem to miss their absent friends or loved ones and didn't question why they never received any word of about them or where they were spending their twilight years.

"Oh, mom, look. Isn't that a sweet sign ...and look, even the baby signed with his footprint."

"Yes, it's sweet." She reluctantly followed her daughter into the hall, which was actually a large room with banquet tables now decorated in her honor.

The food was good, although she didn't taste much of it, the stories were funny and brought back a lot of memories, but then that made her cry, because she was leaving her life for a life unknown or maybe, no life at all. She received lots of cards and hugs and kisses, but strangely, not many tears of sorrow from those she was leaving behind. It was almost as if they had all accepted the *Law of Retirement*, with no questions, no hesitation, and no grief; as she had. This situation just didn't feel... *right*. Was she the only one in the world that questioned the Law? Was she the only one in the world that was frightened of what *Retirement* could possible mean?

She didn't want to retire! She didn't want to leave her house to the State! She didn't want her niece or cousin handling her personal belongings or fighting over the silverware! This wasn't a retirement celebration... this was a *funer*al!

She began to panic and looked for a way out of the hall. She needed to escape. They were not taking her, she would refuse to go.

Searching the hall, she realized there was no way out. Stationed at all three exits were strangers to her. Although, they seemed cordial and spoke to her friends and with familiarity, she didn't know them. They were guards, obviously, but why were guards at a celebration, if no one ever tried to escape? She wanted to put her theory to the test and approached the main entrance and exit. She watched the man closely. Very subtly the stranger stepped directly to the middle of the doorframe- arms folded, legs apart. She turned and headed to the back exit, again keeping a close watch on the man at the door. Once again, as she neared the exit, the man stepped into the center- arms folded, legs apart.

Her theory had been correct! These strange men were guarding the doors to keep her from escaping before she had a chance to consider another tactic, her daughter was at her side.

"Mother, the bus is here. It's time to go."

At first the words didn't register in her panicked brain, until she watched as each of the singular guards became a group of three, at her side. They had known she was thinking of escape and they were here to make sure that didn't happen.

Her daughter stepped up onto a platform and held her hand up to silence the crowd of well-wishers.

"May I please have your attention? The bus is here, and mother's *Retirement* adventure is about to begin. I am so jealous, and I bet there are loads of family and friends who wish it were them."

Listening to the words her daughter had spoken, she muttered under her breath, "I wish it were them, also."

Her daughter was spoke to one of the guards and then turned to her, "It's time to go. Are you ready? Where's your bag?"

She was only able to point; no words would form in her dry mouth. Her daughter called to her grandchildren.

"Children, come give grandma a hug and kiss goodbye." Her two much-loved grandchildren ran and grabbed onto her. They seemed to be the only ones genuinely sorry she was leaving. She gave them a kiss and a hug, and then one of the guards escorted her out of the building as the onlookers waved and wished her farewell. She stepped up onto the bus and stumbled into the first empty seat she saw. She couldn't even wave back at the crowd outside. The large sign was already being pulled down and before the bus left the curb, the crowd was thinning until only her daughter and grandchildren were left, waving. Her daughter mouthed the words, "Write to me as soon as you get there! I love you, Mom!"

The bus door closed and scooted away from the curb and onto the street. She felt as if she was going to vomit.

Inside the bus was cool and fragrant with the smell of lavender. The seats were plush, and she felt herself relax. She looked around at the rest of the passengers. Why... there sat Mrs. Copeland, her daughter's fifth grade teacher... and Harry, the man from her favorite bakery. She didn't feel so alone anymore. She noticed all the passengers relax and she even got a slight smile from Harry. She smiled back, but stayed quiet. None of the *just turned sixty* crowd, spoke. Soft music played in the background and before she knew it, she had fast asleep.

She didn't know how long she'd slept, but awoke when the bus came to a stop. Sitting up and looking around, she noticed the scenery was very familiar. This was her street, and there was her house- looking new and refreshed. The bus doors opened, and someone entered and walking directly to her.

"Sweetie, I've been waiting for you. You're home. Are you ready to begin your *retirement* with me?" This man, this person who was speaking to her...was her husband. It couldn't be! He had died years ago. She must still be sleeping.

"No, dear, you're not sleeping. It is really me and I've come to take you to our home." This specter gestured to the house, they had moved in together, over forty years ago.

She rose slowly and allowed him to lead her from the bus and into her light and bright living room. All her belongings were back in their correct places. Everything was neat and shiny and new.

Her husband placed his arms around her waist and for the first time in so many years she felt completely contented. He guided her to the sofa and past the hall mirror, where she caught a quick glimpse of her reflection. She looked young, just as she had on the day she had married.

Her husband held her closely and whispered, "Welcome to *retirement. I've* already mailed a postcard to our family and friends, telling them you've arrived safe and sound. Now, we can begin our life again and this time we'll be together...forever."

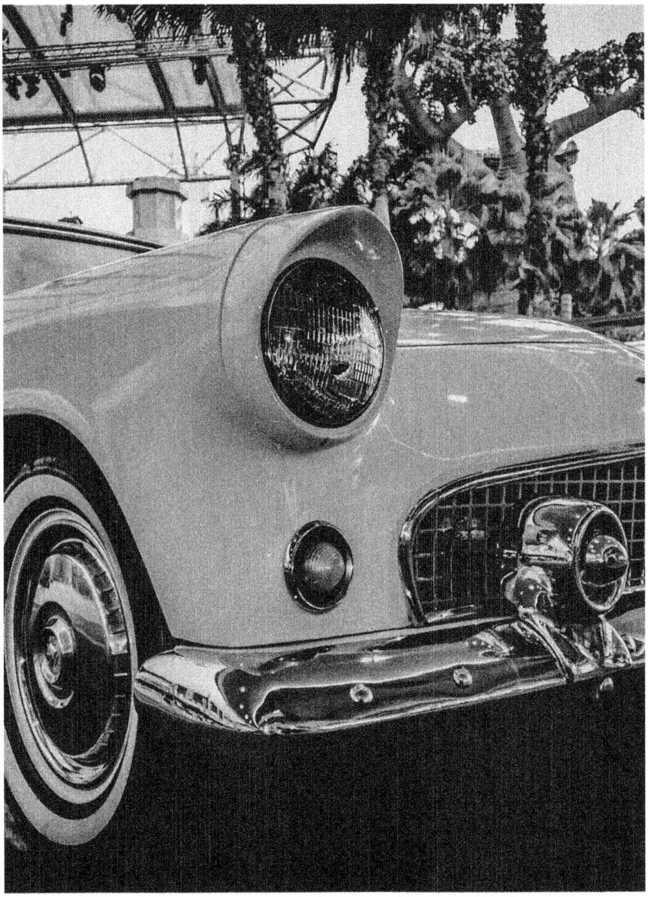

The Bully

Everyone knows one, all towns have them, and all schools have one in every class. You know what I'm referring to of course; *the bully*! Yes, we all know about bullies. They are usually guys, but not always, large, very weak in the IQ department, and usually come from a more dysfunctional family than yours.

This is the tale of a bully, but not the "usual" bully just described. This is about Randall Whitesleeve, the mayor's son, captain of the football team, member of the National Honor Society, President of the senior class, letterman sweater type, king of the prom, and mustang convertible owner. Everything all the girls wanted combined into one tall, dark, hunky body of a .... *bully.*

Randall was like a present your Great-Aunt would send; beautiful wrapping but once ripped off, what was left, was a pair of mittens; poorly knitted. Randall collected friends like someone else collected bottle caps and those friends were just disposable.

If there was no more use, there would be no more friend. Randall was this way since infancy; throwing away his old toys and demanding new. Nothing was special to him; not toys, or clothes, or people. Randall saw and gratified only himself and he became the worst bully the town ever knew.

Randall had all the grown-ups fooled. They worshipped him, swooned and gushed over him, believed every word he uttered. They said nothing but wonderful things about his future. Randall was going to be a success. After all, they were the adults; they knew because they had experienced life.

Randall had no one his age fooled, unless you were a new student, then it took a little longer; possibly a month or maybe a week, or sometimes 24 hours. The kids tried to warn the adults, but they refused to hear anything negative about him. Randall was what all the adults had wanted to be and through him, they would live vicariously.

Randall got through his years of elementary, middle, and now high school with straight A's. In elementary school, he did most of the work himself, until he reached fourth grade. Randall was naturally bright, but he was also naturally lazy. In fourth grade, he sorted out the good from the bad, the pretty from the plain, and the smart from the dull. He was very adept at reading a person's characteristics and began to use this gift to his advantage.

A pretty, little rosy-cheeked classmate, Susie, was extremely popular with the boys, and the girls. Randall knew he could become popular if he hung around her. He did, and he was immediately marked as one of the "popular kids". He stayed Susie's friend until his popularity exceeded hers and he moved on to greener pastures, leaving Susie behind, wondering what she did wrong.

A very plain fourth grade girl with glasses and freckles, Randall soon pegged as the brightest in the class. Randall befriended Mary, in private only; he could not be seen with her in public or he would be marked as a geek. The entire fourth grade year, Mary did Randall's homework, book reports, and allowed him to cheat off of her tests (Randall manipulated the teacher to move his seat right next to Mary's'), until one day when Mary's and Randall's test answers were exactly alike; spelling, phrasing, and sentence structure.

Miss Hipple called them both to her desk. She questioned each one extensively, and then gave Mary an "F" for cheating. Miss Hipple promptly moved Mary to the back of the class giving the child an empty hole in her heart and stomach. She never got an F before and her parents would be furious; especially her father, who expected perfection; always!

The next morning as Mary took her seat, no one questioned the black and swollen eye or the dark circles under them, or even her repaired glasses. Yes, sir, Randall was on his way to stardom.

This kind of behavior was always in Randall's mixed bag of tricks as he traveled through his grade school and middle school years. Randall snagged the prettiest girls to date, the strongest guys to hang out with, and the smartest geeks to do his work. The only thing Randall ever did for himself was sleep, eat, drive too fast, and party too hard.

Randall's class finally reached their senior year and was applying for colleges. Randall had Annabelle fill his application out for him, while he played a video game and ate cookies, in her bedroom. Annabelle was at the top of the class, only exceeded by Randall Whitesleeve, who was at the very tip- top.

Randall was stupid. He knew he'd never get away with the homework stuff unless he had different geeks for each subject. Annabelle was his latest accomplishment. She wrote all his speeches on the ruse of being his "public relations" advisor. It was working out very well, but this was the end of the year and Annabelle had gone far above his expectations. Not only did she write his speeches, complete all applications, but she let him go all the way.

Annabelle worshiped the ground Randall walked on. She questioned him only about not being seen in public with her. His excuse was an overbearing father who wanted no headlines to spoil his political career; and so, Annabelle bought the fabrication- hook, line, and sinker. She loved him, after all; she had given herself to him and he said that she was his first, also. She wasn't, but he needed her at that moment- and anytime he could get it, he wouldn't turn it down. He could always close his eyes and pretend she was Molly, his current girlfriend; who would never let him get to first base.

Annabelle finished his applications and placed them each in their corresponding envelopes, addressed and stamped them, and handed them to Randall.

"Hey, babe, I'm late for football practice. Could you drop them off at the post office for me? Thanks, babe. Catch you later." He didn't wait for Annabelle to reply and he closed the door, leaving her behind; not realizing this would be the last time he would be in her bedroom. Her worth was completed, and she was no longer of any use.

Annabelle sat alone at her desk, pen in hand, and scrawled a note to her parents. She then took her old jump rope and looped one end through the shower bar and the other around her neck. That was the way Annabelle's parents found her. They had no one to blame, as she never, *ever* implicated Randall in anything. In fact, Annabelle's parents did not even know that Randall had been her friend and her lover. Her note merely stated she *felt she had no future, no friends, and could no longer cope in a world that considered her an outcast. She loved them both. Goodbye.*

Annabelle's funeral took place the following week. There were seventeen classmates in attendance, a few teachers, and her mourning family, of course. Randall was swimming at the Club with Molly. He would never know of Annabelle's pregnancy and her family would never guess the father's identity.

Randall had a couple of hanging-out buddies who had been close for a few years. He used them to get into the best circles of people, he used them to be seen with, and he really didn't care about *any of them*. He kept a couple of geeky guys on notice, also. Clarence did all his math, geometry, and physics work. Ernie fixed his car, just for the fun of it, and Lester did all his woodshop refinishing. What a nice bunch of guys! Losers, actually; to Randall.
Randall had no more use for Clarence and had stood him up several times in the past three days and consequently, Clarence stopped making "Randall Plans" and Captain Kirk became his best friend; once again.

Randall hadn't been seen with Lester for at least a month, in fact, no one had been seen with Lester for at least a month; not his parents, not his sister, not his teachers or classmates. Lester seemed to have vanished off the face of the earth. Randall was getting really pissed at Lester's family. They kept calling him and asking when he had last seen Lester. He had already told them!
God, people were so annoying and whiney!

Ernie would be the last to bite the dust, but not until he had given Randall's Mustang a thorough going over. Randall couldn't afford to have his status symbol break down at college; now could he? Ernie was still on the string Randall was pulling.
Randall couldn't wait to get away from this little hick town. His father was delusional about his political career, his mother was a drunk, and his sister...well let's just say she had an awful lot of notches on her belt.

Tonight was the prom, he would be elected King and Molly, Queen. That was a fact-not a belief. It was all arranged; a little extortion went a long way to getting what you wanted. If he was really lucky, he could get it from Molly and if not, there was always someone waiting in the wings to spread her legs for him.

In two days he would graduate at the top of his class. He would accept all his awards with graciousness, and recite his Valedictorian's speech with great pomp and circumstance. He would let his classmates and those ignorant adults know that, "*he was their future.*"

The next day, Randall woke up with a horrific hangover and no memory of the after-prom party. Hell, he wasn't even sure how he had gotten to his own house or his bed. One of his *friends* must have delivered him to the correct address. All Randall had to do now was wait for graduation and then he was out of this place!
Randall spent most of that day in his room or his bathroom.

That evening, feeling much better, he decided to take the Mustang for a cruise. Not bothering to ask permission or simply say he was going out; he left. His parents didn't much care where he went or what he did, as long as he was the *golden boy* and didn't embarrass them. They had high hopes in Randall. He was going to be the one from this town who would make it in the *big time!*

He didn't bother calling any of the guys or any of the girls. He didn't need any of them anymore. He wouldn't need anyone until he hit the college campus, then he would assess his prospects. Oh, life was so *damn good*! He drove around the small town, waving haphazardly to those who called his name or honked their horns at him. His cell phone rang. Oh, shit- Lester's parents! He disconnected the call.

Randall decided to pull into McDonald's for a coke. He had ordered and was just about to pull around to the pay-window, when he heard a honk behind him. He nonchalantly glanced into his rear-view mirror. He couldn't quite see who was driving, but there was a girl in the passenger seat, waving like crazy at him. He ignored the interruption, paid, and pulled up to the pick-up window. The car honked its horn and once again Randall saw a woman waving at him.

"Oh, hell; whatever!" Randall sort of saluted with two fingers into the mirror at the car, retrieved his soda, and drove quickly out of the parking lot. Glancing back, Randall saw that the car was not following him, and he put his mind into cruise control. He was enjoying the night far too much to be annoyed by a honking horn and a crazy broad.

Randall decided to head out of town to the quarry, where the geeks and losers hung out and went swimming. Anyone, whose families could not afford the Country Club, would swim at the quarry. Normally, he would have gone to the club, but it was well after hours.

Swimming was not permitted in the quarry, but kids had been ignoring that warning for over fifty years and no one had ever gotten hurt. Randall just wanted a cool, quiet place to think about his next move in life, he had no intention of swimming. Most of the kids that hung out at the quarry would already be at home and safely tucked into their little beddies. He'd probably have the place to himself. He floored the machine. The faster he could get to his destination, the better he'd feel. He rounded a curve, tires squealing on the blacktop, and began the descent toward the quarry.

A movement out of the corner of Randall's eye, from the backseat, caught his attention. For a moment, he actually believed he saw Lester and Annabelle sitting on his black leather seats. Randall blinked, and they disappeared. He began to laugh, out loud.

"Hey, Randall, old boy, get a grip! You're seeing things, man." He shook his head to clear the cobwebs and then laughed, "That would be totally impossible! You know those two won't be back, again!"

Another movement and then a cold hand on his neck startled Randall, and his foot accelerated the car as it headed for the quarry. He tried to take his foot from the gas pedal, but it was stuck. The last sound Randall heard, before his car hit the surface of the murky water was a young woman's voice, which sounded a whole lot like Annabelle.

"I loved you and you used me. Aren't you ashamed of yourself?"

The police wrecker crew pulled the Mustang out of the quarry on graduation day. They all shook their heads in disbelief at discovering Randall's body still buckled in behind the steering wheel. It was if there had been no attempt to escape. The police also found no brake marks on the macadam, except the rubber laid during the curve about a half -mile from the hill running toward the quarry. The obvious conjecture was, that the boy was going *fast-extremely fast.*

The townsfolk all wondered how such an accident could have happened to their *Golden Boy.* They uttered phrases like, what a shame, what a useless death, what a waste, why him of all people? These were the thoughts of the adults, what the kids were thinking? Well, who knows.

That night at the graduation ceremony there were three empty chairs placed upon the outdoor stage. One of the chairs held a large bouquet of roses, the other two had smaller bunches of wildflowers. The Student Master of Ceremonies
rose to speak. He motioned to the three empty chairs and cleared his throat.

"Tonight, before we begin our speeches and our journey into the future, let us remember those who are no longer with us; Lester Martin, Annabelle Taylor, and Randall Whitesleeve. May Lester and Annabelle rest in peace...yes, and Randall. Let us pray."

While the minister chanted his long-winded prayer about the goodness of those that had past and the hope for the future generation, the student who ranked fourth in the graduating class took a quick look at his notes. Ernie jabbed him in his side to tell him the prayer was over, and he was up.

"Clarence, it's time for your speech, man. Get on up there!"

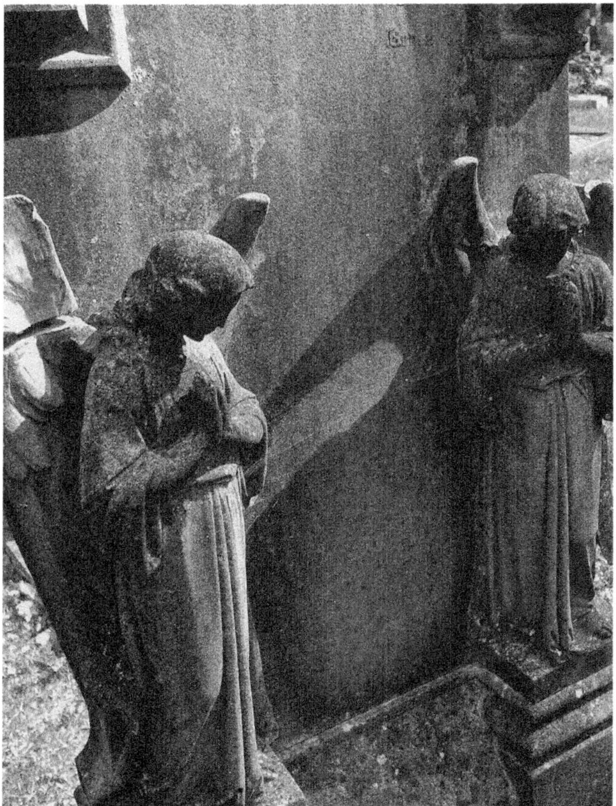

I'll Be Back for You

Coming home, after the funeral, Ernie Lazarus threw his hat on the well-worn sofa and pulled at his, much too tight, tie. He slumped into *his* chair and gazed around the empty, but tidy front room of the run-down house. Picking up a beer can, he shook it, and realizing it was empty, threw the can across the room.

"Get me another, beer!" He hollered and then slowly rose from the chair and sauntered into the kitchen. Opening the refrigerator door, he grabbed a beer and determined he'd have to get a case or two; he was getting low.

"That *bitch*, didn't even get more beer before she went and killed herself!"

Ernie was having a little trouble remembering the night Rose died, in fact, several times he had yelled for her to get him something before he remembered she was never going to get him anything again.

"That bitch was never any good, anyways." Ernie muttered.

Those were Ernie's feelings and no one else's. Had you inquired about the character of Rose Lazarus to any of the townsfolk, you'd receive a glowing report about a hard-working, self-sacrificing, and kind-hearted person.

Ernie's character, on the other hand, was quite the opposite. Ernie was a lazy drunkard, who could not keep a job, was too lazy to keep up with the once pretty, little house and a wife beater. Everyone in town knew it, but no one ever did anything to change it, and met her death at Ernie's hand, or I should say...foot.

The official Coroner's report stated: *Accidental Death caused by fall down flight of stairs in deceased's own home. Injuries: three broken ribs, fractured tibia, fractured skull and broken neck.*

Although the Coroner and the town's lawmen did not believe it had been an accident, there was no proof otherwise. No one believed that Rose fell on her own accord and it was reminiscent of the time, ten years prior, when Rose lost her baby. Ernie told the doctor Rose had tripped over her own clumsy feet, and fallen down the same flight of stairs which would eventually take her life. On that particular night, the fall only killed the baby. Ernie was grateful for the loss. Rose was devastated. Ernie made sure she didn't get pregnant again. He took her by force when he wanted to and he made sure to beat any little snot-nosed brat out of her, just in case.

Everyone in town knew Rose was not a clumsy girl. She was the life of the party only a few years before. She could dance all night long and all the boys in town pursued her affections. Rose was a petite girl, but strong with soft brown hair and beautiful green eyes. She was one of the prettiest girls for miles around. She was always smiling; *then*. Her smiling slowed down the day after her wedding to Ernie and neighbors never saw that smile again after she lost the baby.

The young men that dated or hung around Rose, never understood why she would choose a waste of a man like Ernie Lazarus, over any one of them. Ernie often bragged that he could have had any girl he'd wanted, whether he loved them or not. Rose was a challenge for Ernie and once he'd won, there was no more challenge.

Ernie's mother was a mean and hard-hearted woman, except when it came to Ernie. Old Mrs. Lazarus hated the mere sight of Rose and kept up a constant negative prattle about her to her son. If Rose ever said anything derogatory against Ernie, Mamma had a hissy-fit.

One spring day, after Ernie had been whining about the loss of his fifth job and Mamma was watching Rose hang up the washing, Rose shook her head and told Ernie to stop his drinking and maybe he'd hold onto a job for more than two weeks.

Mamma was over at the wash line in a flash and slapped Rose across the face so hard, it caused her to stumble backwards and twist her ankle, "You don't know nothing about my boy, even if you are married to him. He doesn't have a strong constitution for laboring. He's more the thinking kind. Now you, you're as healthy as a horse and God know'd it. That's why you gotta take care of my boy. You watch your harsh mouth around him!" With another killer glare, Mamma strode off and up the road to her own run-down shack.

Rose was just picking herself up from the ground when she felt a heavy blow across her back and once again, she fell forward. "Don't you ever speak to me like that again in front of Mamma or anybody else, for that matter!" He gave her hip a swift hard kick and staggered to sleep off the beer.

Rose waited for eighteen years for Ernie's thinking strength to kick in, but it never did. The last ten years of her life, she became robotic. Get up in the morning, clean the house, cook breakfast for Ernie, wash up and change into her waitress uniform.

During the days, six days a week, Rose was a waitress down at the County Line Restaurant. Around four in the afternoon, she'd hurry home to make Ernie's supper and get herself ready for her second job at the Pin Point Bowling Lanes. She worked every weekday evening until ten at the Lanes. By the time she got home, she was completely wiped out and Ernie was completely drunk.

He'd never leave her alone to just go to bed. He was constantly trying to pick a fight, so she couldn't go upstairs.

Something was always wrong with her cooking or she didn't wash his best shirt that day or she hadn't stocked up on beer. If she tried to defend herself, his answer was always a punch in the face or the stomach or a kick on the back of her legs. Rose prayed for the nights Ernie was too drunk to get himself home.

After she lost the baby, her life really meant nothing to her and now after living with the monster for eighteen years she finally had enough.

The day of her *accident* she called her older sister up in Ashville and asked if she could come and stay with her just until she could get on her feet, again. Coral was more than happy to welcome Rose; she'd nagged Rose to leave Ernie for years.

Rose gathered only one small bag of clothing and the jar of money she hid from her husband. She had almost seven-hundred dollars, and that was going to give her the courage to buy a bus ticket and start over in Ashville.

She set her bag behind the bush in their small front yard and hurried into the house to make Ernie's favorite supper, fried chicken, biscuits, and gravy. Rose waited and waited for Ernie to come home, but she knew her bus would leave in an hour and had to get to the station. Writing a quick note, telling Ernie she was leaving, she opened the front door, hoisted her bag, and started down the road toward the bus station.

A hand grabbed her bag and swung her around, "Where you think you're goin' Rose?" Ernie asked in a drunken slur.

"I'm leaving you, Ernie. I'm going to stay with my sister in Ashville," she replied.

"Leavin' me, are you? Leavin' me? I should be the one leavin' you, you bitch," he shouted.

"Stop yelling, Ernie, you'll wake up the neighbors," Rose begged.

"What the hell do I care if the neighbors wake up? They'll find out what a bitch you are for leavin' me."

"Ernie, *you're* the laughing stock of this neighborhood and the town. Now, let go of my bag and let me leave!" Rose tried to yank free.

Ernie held onto the bag, in a bear-like grip, and as Rose tried to tug on the handle, the suitcase opened. All of Rose's contents fell onto the muddy road along with the jar of money. Ernie's eyes fell upon the jar and grabbed it up before Rose had a chance to turn around.

"Ernie, that's *mine!*"

Ernie held the jar up to the street lamp, "You holding out on me, Rose?"

Ernie turned and ran back to the house with Rose in pursuit.

"I earned that money! It's mine!" Rose demanded.

"*I earned that money, it's mine",* mimicked Ernie. He tried to close the door before Rose could get in, but because of his drinking, his reactions were a bit slower than usual and Rose was able to push him away and enter. Ernie raced up the stairs and Rose followed. Stopping at the stairwell, at the top, Rose tried to reason with her drunken husband.
"Please, Ernie, give me back my money and I'll leave and you'll never see me again."

"Oh, you can leave, but not with this." He held up the jar to the bare light bulb. "How much is in here, anyway, Rose?" Ernie eyed the jar with greed.

"It's none of your business! That money is mine, not yours. I saved it from all those years of working just to keep you in *booze*! Give it back to me, Ernie!"

"What did you say? You givin' orders now, Rose? I don't think so," he glowered at her.

Rose reached for the money jar when Ernie raised his foot and kicked her out of the way.

"You go ahead and leave, bitch, but I keep the money!"

Rose, caught off balance from his kick, tumbled backwards down the flight of stairs. Ernie stood rooted and then staggered to her still body. "You dumb, bitch! Now look what you done! They'll think it was me and not your clumsy big feet!"

A hand grabbed his trouser leg and a whisper of a voice tried to speak. Ernie looked down and realized Rose was not dead, but she was close to it and was trying to say something to him. He leaned closer to catch the soft words. *"I'll be back for you. Mark my words, Ernie. I'll be back for you."* Rose sighed and then was still. Ernie raced out of the house and straight to the police. Rose's death grasp had scared the drunkenness right out of him.

Ernie told everyone it was an accident and they had bought it or pretended to. Today though, at the funeral, no one had said any words of condolence to him. He was surprised how many people were in the cemetery to see Rose lowered into the ground. He didn't know that many people existed and wondered why they all came. *Couldn't have come just to pay respect to Rose. She wasn't anything special; was she?*

At home now, Ernie picked up the jar that sat on the end table beside the chair, unscrewed the lid, and began to count the money. "That damn bitch had over seven-hundred dollars saved," he thought. Draining the can of beer, he leaned back and made plans about how to spend his new-found wealth. Eventually he fell asleep.

Waking up in total darkness, Ernie swore he heard a familiar voice whisper in his ear.

"Umph...wha'...who's there?" Peering around the room, he seemed to see shadows in every corner, movement behind each curtain. For the first time in his life, Ernie Lazarus was frightened. He didn't know why; it was something he felt. He tried to stand and kicked something hard at his feet.

The money jar rolled across the braided rug, making a clinking noise, as the coins fell from one side to the other. "What the hell...?"

"I told you this was mine, Ernie. You had no right taking my money."

"Who said that?" Ernie swung his head from side to side trying to see through the blackness. "Ben Jackson, you playing tricks on me? Come on out now and I'll forget about that hundred you owe me."

"Ben's not here, Ernie. It's just you and me. Now, I want my jar of money and I want you to go to the police chief and tell him what really happened here last week."

"What happened? Nothing happened. Rose accidentally fell down the stairs; you know how clumsy she could be. Come on now, Ben, Herb, enough of the jokes, "he sputtered.

"Ernie Lazarus, this is no joke! I've come back for my money and my freedom. You kept me like a slave for too long! You made me lose my baby! You hit me, humiliated me and went through all the money I earned like it was water. I want my money back!"

"You can't be Rose. You're dead!" Ernie's eyes scanned the room, "I'm drunk and you're dead and you can't spend money where you're going, I might as well just keep it, huh, clumsy Rose! You kill yourself and you blame it on me!"

"Ernie, you're right. I can't spend the money anymore, but you aren't going to spend it, either."

"Oh, get out of my head. You're just the last swig of the beer I drank. I'm going to bed, and when I wake up you'll be gone!" Ernie picked up the money jar and began climbing the steps to the upstairs bedroom. As he reached the landing, at the top, a vision of Rose floated in front of him. He blinked his eyes and shook his head.

"I told you, Ernie. I told you I would be back for you."

Before Ernie had a chance to take one more step, the jar flew out of his arms and shattered on the stairs. Clinking coins bounced from step to step on their way to the main floor. Ernie reached out to grab the jar before it fell, lost his balance, and tumbled head-first following the coins on their downward journey. He lay on the linoleum floor, head to one side at a very peculiar angle, legs bent unnaturally under his hips.

Yep, it was a very nasty *accidental* fall…I'd say.

Epilogue

The seven-hundred dollars paid for Ernie's funeral costs. He couldn't be laid out beside Rose since she bought herself a plot. Rose may not have escaped from Ernie in life, but at least in death she was laid to rest whole acre away. Things have a way of working out sometimes.
Not many people showed up for Ernie's burial, Ben, Herb, the beer distributor's salesman, the burly bartender at the Corner Bar, and the minister's assistant. The minister was fulfilling a previous engagement with his fishing pole and sent his assistant to officiate. The ceremony was of no length, there were no flowers, no singing, no weeping, no words of condolences, only an empty beer can tossed into the hole by one of the mourners.

It seemed a fitting tribute. Don't y'all think?

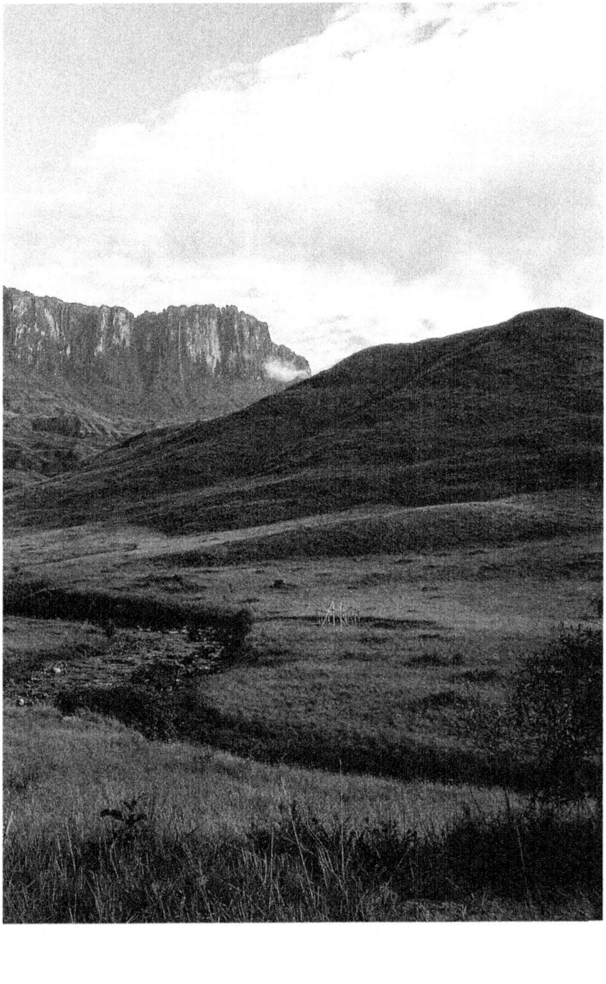

The Massacre

It was a beautiful autumn day. The grasses on the rolling hills waved in the crisp breeze, the sun played peeka-boo with the clouds and we felt wonderfully exhilarated by the change from the sticky summer heat to the refreshing autumn breezes.

Because of the brightness of the day and our good mood, the entire family decided to wander the hills and valleys together, stopping to eat lunch near a Lodgepole pine and take a cool refreshing drink from the lake. Cousins, aunts, uncles, brothers, sisters, parents, grandparents, we were all there down to the newest newborn. There must have been one-hundred of us at least.

The young ones romped and chased one another, squealing in delight when caught. The young adult couples watched their little ones playing, always keeping a close watch, for snakes and other dangers.

It was the year 1870, and the wildlife was rampant here in the mountains and canyons of Wyoming. A parent needed to be very alert and protective of their children in this kind of environment.

Some of the older members of the family went to lie down under a shady pine at the base of a nearby mountain. Sometimes, when we'd come here, we'd watch the climbers struggle up the sides of the tall and snow-capped mountains. Our family had no desire to struggle up the sides of mountains or lie in the hot springs all day; although the older ones did enjoy an occasional soak or two. The hot water seemed to relieve the frequent aches and pains of age.

That day, some of us decided to take a walk up to the next ledge, to see if the Lupine flowers were growing. As we approached the ridge, there was a deafening sound, just below us. Maybe there was a stampede! Our children were down there and amid those frantic hooves!

We hurried to look toward the valley, no stampeding herd, but about fifty men on horseback, thundered into our valley, holding metal sticks.
When a metal stick gave a terrible *BOOM*, one of our family members dropped. What was happening? What had we done to deserve this?

Those of us on the ridge ran as fast as we could to gather our loved ones for safety. We needed to surround the little ones. They were our future!

The metal sticks kept booming and our members kept falling, blood running like rivers. In our confusion and fear, we knew we had to do something, but were no match for the metal sticks. Our children were trying to escape, but all around them the adults fell, and blood splattered.

The children were crying, calling for their parents for protection- but they were no more parents, except for those of us on the ridge. I saw my twins, running in circles as three men surrounded them. I let out an angry cry and ran as fast as I could to get there. As I came close, I witnessed one of the men draw a knife and walk to one of my fallen little ones.

I have never felt such rage, and I attacked the man, causing him to stumble forward. My actions brought out the frenzy in those men and their metal sticks were again being fired, as fast as they could get them raised into the air.

When one of us fell, the men on horses whooped and hollered; as if it were a conquest.

We faced the men on horseback with pride and strength, while trying to hold our grief under control. If we had met one of those men by themselves, we would have prevailed, but there were too many of them and too many metal sticks.

A final crack of the metal stick is all I heard, and I dropped to my knees, bleeding profusely dying.

"That's all of them! We're bound to win the competition this year! God, that was exhilarating!"

"How many does that make, Lem?"

"One-hundred seventy-two- not counting the eighty-six we killed this morning."

"What are we gonna do with the carcasses, Joe?"

"We don't need nothing but the tongues, for a head count. Just let the rest of the body for those bone-picking vultures to eat."

"Hey! Clarence just came in and said there were at least four to five-hundred *buffalo, in the next valley!"

"Let's ride, boys!"

The men finished taking their trophies, mounted their horses and rode off; with lots of loud and delighted cheering.

*Footnote: In the beginning of the 1800's, 75 million buffalo roamed The Great Plains. Because of the railroad expansion and the European migration, contests were held to see who could slaughter the most buffalo. In 1870, those numbers were reduced to only 540 buffalo and by the beginning of the 1900's, only a few dozen existed.

The "white" man did not use any part of the buffalo and let their bodies rot all over the plains. The tongue was cut out to prove the number of buffalo killed. In the 1900's, Congress realized its mistake and placed the buffalo under its protection. Soon the buffalo began to thrive, again. However, today most of the buffalo are raised on ranches for meat and hides. In Yellowstone National Park, 3,000 buffalo still roam freely.

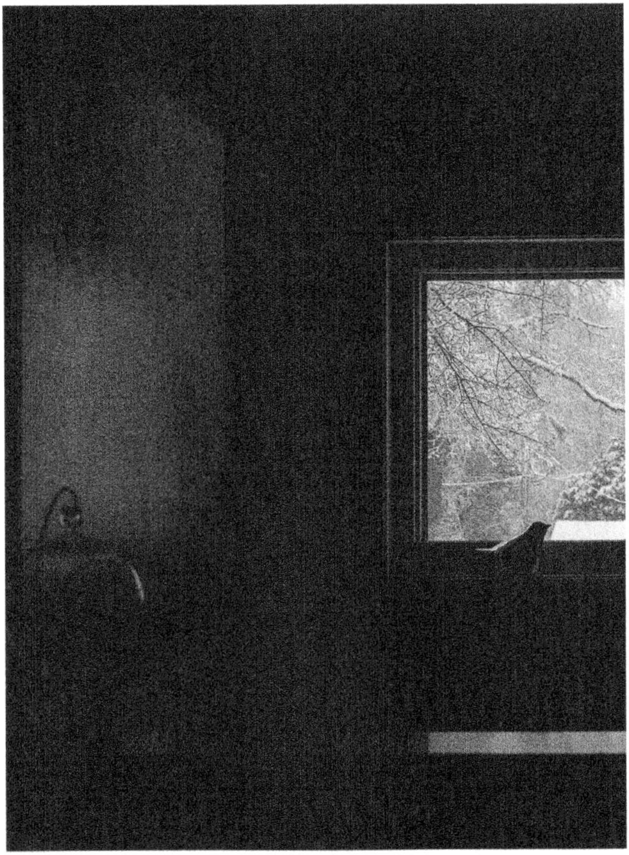

Sunshine, Scallops, and Suicide

"What a wonderful morning", she thought, as she climbed out of bed. With so much to get done today, she needed to get started.

After dressing, she called her friend, Mary, to make a date for breakfast. They were to meet in twenty minutes at the local diner.

Up until today, she had been on sort of a diet, but this morning she was going to order eggs, sausage, bacon, and home fries. Her mouth watered just thinking about it.

Breakfast had lived up to her expectations and the pleasant conversation with Mary, exceeded it. She and Mary hugged their goodbyes and she drove to the nearest plus-sized women's clothing store. She wanted to purchase a white cotton nightgown. She knew exactly what she wanted. The nightgown would be long, with long or medium length sleeves; she hated her flabby arms, and an eyelet around the neckline. After hunting for almost an hour, she finally found a gown similar to vision.

Her last two stops would be to the supermarket and to the video store. She wanted to make a good meal for dinner and watch a couple of her favorite movies.

She purchased some votive candles and bath bubbles, as well as fresh haddock, scallops, and shrimp. She would broil the seafood in a garlic sauce and serve it alongside some rice pilaf and a salad.

She was feeling so good, things were going her way today She couldn't believe her luck, when she found, *Pride & Prejudice* and all of the *Twilight* movies available at the video store. She planned to stay up late, after taking a luxurious bubble bath, watch all the movies she had and the *Harry Potter* movies she owned; all eight of them.

Well, into the afternoon, she arrived back home and started on the preparations, before the evening's festivities. After marinating the seafood, she straightened up her house, put fresh sheets on the bed, did her wash, including the new nightgown because she hated scratchy clothing, and wrote and mailed some correspondence she had put off.

The house was sparkling and shiny clean, her seafood was placed under the broiler, the salad was made and chilling, rice pilaf in the microwave and six or seven cans of diet coke were in the fridge.

After dinner was finished cooking, she took her movies into her bedroom and popped *Pride & Prejudice* into the DVD player. She always cried over this movie and tonight was no exception. She ate slowly while she watched.

Feeling stiff from lying in bed so long, she took her dirty dishes to the sink to wash and then headed into the bathroom to draw herself a nice hot bath. She poured an abundant amount of bubble bath under the flowing water from the faucet. While waiting for the tub to fill, she lit six candles and placed them around the bath, then went to lock the doors and check the windows. *"All battened down"*, she thought.

She gathered her cold sodas, a bucket of ice, a fancy wine glass, and other necessary items and placed them on the nightstand or on the floor beside her bed. Taking her new nightgown from the drawer and a new pair of soft white socks, she entered the bathroom, took off her dirty clothing and stepped into the tub.

"Ah-h-h, that feels so good". She laid her head back on her inflatable stick-on pillow and closed her eyes. The fragrance of the bubble bath and the warmth of the water relaxed her, and she allowed her mind to wander into realms she had refused to think about all day.

This life she was living was not the one she wanted. Ever since she was a child, all she ever dreamed about was a husband, a home of her own, and children. She had gotten all of that, but then something went terribly wrong. After thirty years of marriage, the husband walked out on her and the children and grandchildren. Her health deteriorated, and she had to resign her teaching position. She lost her house and her car and her self-respect. In the meantime, her ex-husband was living the *Life of Riley* with his new and wealthy wife.

She had to depend on her children for support. Even though she was bringing in social security, there was not enough for her to live independently. She was becoming a burden to her children, and she did not want that.

She was very lonely and realized that she had never known *real* love from a man. She reasoned that her ex-husband wanted to get away from his over-suffocating parents and then after so many years, she just became the lesser of two evils. Then he met his current wife over the internet. With her, he wouldn't have to struggle to make ends meet, he could do what he wanted so he walked away from all those years of family.

It had been over ten years since she had relaxed into a loving embrace from a man, or held someone's hand, and she really had no one to talk to. Her children were busy with their own troubles and lives and her mother had changed a lot over the past few years. The only thing she felt needed for, was to clean house which she didn't do well enough for her daughters, take care of their kids, which she also didn't do well enough for her daughters, and cook. Those were the only things left in her life; except for reading about and watching movies about true love, *forever love*. She knew that kind of love never happened in real life, but for an hour or so, she could.

Tomorrow she would be sixty and she knew she could not turn back the clock. She would never be young or have all her teeth again. She knew she'd never be able to see as well or hear as well, as she had at one time. She knew that men were not attracted to her; never were, never would be. She knew her children laughed at her, and talked about her, and didn't think she had very much common sense. She knew they thought they had done lots for her, and she had done nothing for them. She knew they didn't like to hold conversations with her, because everything she said, they contradicted or often said, she *sounded crazy*.

She couldn't even joke around with them as they would tell her she wasn't speaking *appropriately* around the kid. Hell, she couldn't even cry or be depressed if she felt like it.

They were constantly angry with her over something. She didn't wash that coffee cup well enough, she allowed the grandchildren to drink too many sodas, she played too many computer games, she didn't respect other peoples' property, she didn't fold the towels the way she was supposed to, and she didn't act the way a grandmother should act; at least that's what her children thought.

She allowed herself to have a good cry, washed her body and hair, and released the bubbled water. She grabbed a towel and stepping out of the tub, began to rub herself dry. She brushed her hair and pulled the nightgown over her head. She cleaned up the bubbles, still left in the tub, and walked back to her bedroom.

She popped in the first of the *Twilight* movies, filled the wine glass with ice and diet coke and opened the first of the four medication bottles that sat on her nightstand. She popped ten or twelve into her mouth, took a deep swig of the soda, and lay down to watch her movie.

She had no idea how long this would take, but she was ready to watch as many movies and drink as many diet cokes as necessary.

As she swooned over the leading man in *Twilight* like a 13-year-old, her thoughts checked off the day's accomplishments; breakfast with a friend, clean house, great food, wonderful bath, and plenty of pills.

All in all, it had been simply a *glorious* day!

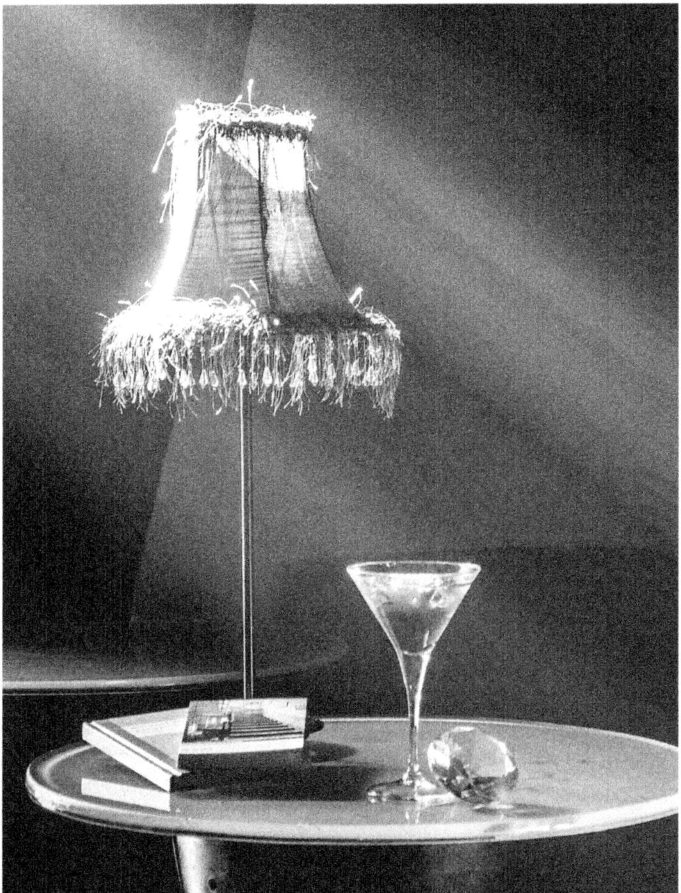

An Evening in Chicago

<u>1928-New Year's Eve</u>

"You've got money in your pocket,
I've got diamonds on my hand.
We have a cottage on the ocean,
With our own private stretch of sand.

My clothes are all Chanel, and
I've got fur coats by galore,
We've got such a rich life.
We couldn't ask for more!

We spend weekends in Havana,
and we've seen every Broadway play.
We ski on the Swiss Alps and we
own a fourteen-room chalet.

Daddy owns some horses
and his Wall Street stock is up.
According to his sources,
his horse will win the Preakness Cup.

Life is grand-life simply soars
We're in love and we have riches,
We just couldn't want for more!"

"Ladies and gentlemen, you have been listening to the newest Lila Lane recording, "*Who Could Want for More?*" on Chicago's WMAQ Radio.

Welcome to <u>An Evening in Chicago</u> with your host, Saul Marvey."

"Good evening, my listening friends. I should have said, Happy New Year's Eve. This is Saul Marvey and we're going to be spending the next few hours with music, exciting friends, and breaking news. This is a countdown of 1928 and tomorrow we'll be looking into the eyes of the last year of this decade. Amazing, isn't it?"

"We have an old friend with us tonight-oops, I should have said a long-time friend, because she's really not that old; until tomorrow."

"Saul, you mean old thing! You know as well as I do, that I'm only going to be twenty-five, tomorrow!"

"Yes, ladies and gentlemen, our special guest, Miss Lila Lane, whose birthday falls on New Year's Day. Lila will be a whopping twenty-five years old, at 12:01am. Welcome back Lila. I'm so glad you could spend New Year's Eve with me and my listening audience. How are you, darling?!

"I'm happy to be here, Saul. Just delighted. You know me Saul; I'm feeling on top of the world!"

"Lila, I hear you're doing a film with Billy Haines? What's it called and when will it be released?"

The film is called, *The Sun of the Desert*, and we're to begin shooting on January fourth and should be completed by the end of March or early April. I am simply so excited and Billy's not bad to look at either, if you know what I mean, Saul!"

"I've also been informed that you have moved to Crystal Lake. Have you given up your home in LA?"

"Oh, Saul, don't be silly. Of course, I still have my home in LA, but Crystal Lake is my get-away place. It's a Cape Cod house surrounded by pines and all kinds of trees. It's simply the *cat's meow*!"

"Is it true, Lila, that Johnny Capella helped you find the place? Isn't Mr. Capella closely watched by the Chicago law officials?"

"Saul! You silly goose! Mr. Capella had the house constructed and merely sold it to me. I even have a pool! Mr. Capella saw to everything."

"Isn't Capella married, Lila?"

"Oh, pooh, it isn't like that, Saul! It's more of a business arrangement and yes, Mr. Capella is married and has three children. I merely bought a house, that's all!"

"Oh, it's time for the countdown, Lila. Let's all count.
Ten...nine...eight...seven...six...five...four...three...two...one! Happy New Year, everyone! Happy 1929, Lila, and to my listening audience and I pray that 1929 will be as great a year for all of us; as was, 1928."

"Happy New Year, Saul!"

"Thanks, Lila. This is Saul Marvey, saying, Good...Evening, Chicago!"

<u>1931-New Year's Eve</u>

*I'll serenade you to dreamland.
I'll sit with you all the while.
I'll hold your hand while you're sleeping.
I'll wake you up with a smile.*

*Although, we've no money to speak of
Every day I thank the Lord up above.
I'll serenade you to dreamland
and we'll get along on our love.*

"Ladies and gentlemen, you have been listening to the newly released, "*I'll Serenade You*" by Lila Lane, on Chicago's first radio station, WMAQ. This is <u>An Evening in Chicago</u> with your host, Saul Marvey!"

"Good evening, Chicago! This is your host, Saul Marvey, saying Happy New Year's Eve. We have lots of music, breaking news, lively conversations, and our New Year's Eve guest, Miss Lila Lane. Happy New Year's Eve, Lila. You're looking absolutely radiant, tonight."

"Thank you, ever so much, Saul and same to you. Although, for most of your listening audience, I suppose this is not going to be a very good year, is it? Much the same as the last three."

"No, I suppose not, but things will change, I can feel it! Let's speak of happier things, Lila. Our listening folks have written in to ask, why a beautiful young woman, such as you, always spends New Year's Eve with us, rather than at a grand party or with some handsome man."

"I'll celebrate later, Saul. I love being with you and your listeners on New Year's Eve and as far as the future; I'd like to spend every New Year's Eve with you all."

"That's wonderful! You have a formal invitation to spend every year with me, here, in our studio. Now, how is that beautiful home in Crystal Lake, Lila?"

"I've had a circular drive added and lots of landscaping to the grounds."

"Listening friends, I know Lila's home is quite beautiful, because I've been there many times, as a guest and friend. Lila throws one heck of a party, folks!"

"Oh, Saul, they are just little get togethers for my friends, but thank you."

"Lila, I've heard you might be opening a club here in Chicago with Johnny Capella. Is that a fact or just a rumor?"

"That is definitely a fact, Saul!"

"Are you giving up the Hollywood life, Lila? It would certainly be our loss if you are."

"Well, to be perfectly honest, Saul, what has happened to Billy Haines has completely devastated me. It's not the same in Hollywood, anymore. Contracts are being bought and sold, good scripts are getting harder to find, and actors fear "lifestyle" leaks and repercussions. I still have a few films to do and when they are finished, I'll be moving back to my hometown of Chicago."

"What about the club, Lila?'

"Mr. Capella and I have decided to become business partners and open up a club in the old Knickerbocker Hotel. It will be called, "*Lila's*". I'll be headlining, and Mr. Capella will focus on the business side, new acts, expenses, all those kinds of things. I'll be developing the acts and the menu. We'll be opening next month, and I'd like you, darling Saul, to be my very special guest that evening."

"I'd love to, Lila. I'll be there! Oh, there's the start of the countdown! Let's go folks, Lila. Ten...nine...eight...seven...six...five...four...three...two...one... Happy New Year everyone and Happy Birthday to you, Lila! Happy 1932 everyone! This has been An Evening in Chicago with me, your host, Saul Marvey - Good...Night!"

1934 - New Year's Eve

"We've got to end this sordid affair,
We've got to cut the cord.
You've got another life out there,
and I can't go on like this anymore!
Our love is always hidden in the shadows.
But there's always someone who sees.
I've given up my life, God knows.
I've got to set my love for you, free!"

"You have been listening to Lila Lane and her new single, *Ending this Affair*.

Good evening ladies and gentlemen, you are welcome to join us with An Evening in Chicago on WMAQ Radio, with your host, Saul Marvey!"

"Happy New Year's Eve, Chicago. Can you believe it, listeners? Tomorrow will be 1935. Quite a lot of things have been going on in our world, some good and some...not so good. One good thing for me tonight is to have the lovely and always delightful, Miss Lila Lane, join us in our New Year's Eve festivities. I haven't seen Lila for so long, now, it
seems ages ago, since we've talked."

"I am always happy to be here with you, Saul. The world certainly has changed in a few short years, hasn't it, folks?"

"How's the club doing, Lila?"

"The club is great, Saul. The Marx Brothers will be there, next week. Their movie, "A Night at the Opera" was such a huge success and they said they'd do me a favor and headline at the club for a few weeks. So, I'm very busy there and abroad. I've just returned from a tour in Europe."

"Wow, Europe! London, Paris, Berlin, I suppose?"

"Yes, my singing tour took me to all those beautiful cities, but Berlin was a very scary place, Saul, and I won't be going back, there, any time soon!"

"Why, for gosh sakes?"

"Well, there is trouble brewing over there. I can feel it! I went to perform at a gala for the new German Chancellor, Adolf Hitler, and he was extremely rude and very frightening!"

"Why, Lila?"

"I don't like the man, Saul! He wouldn't greet me in the receiving line, never applauded after I sang, and I heard him say to a guest, and I am quoting him, 'By the skillful and sustained use of propaganda, one can make a people see even heaven as hell or an extremely wretched life as a paradise.' He's a terrible little man, Saul!"

"Why on earth would anyone ignore you, darling?"

"Because, I'm Jewish! I was told he hates the Jews and plans a propaganda campaign against all the Jewish people in Germany. Oh, no! Forget that last bit of conversation, Saul. That was to be kept strictly confidential and I just blew it...oh, my! Me and my big mouth are now probably in a lot of trouble. Let's talk about something else, shall we, Saul?"

"Of course, Lila. Let's talk about your lovely home in Crystal Lake. I haven't been a guest there in quite a while. What's new in Crystal Lake, Lila?"

"I've had a top floor bedroom suite added for myself. The house has been under construction lately and I haven't had many guests. But I will soon, Saul."

"I've been hearing that John Capella has been doing a lot of his business at your home. I've also heard that he has been associated with the Chicago Mafia and one, Mr. John Dillinger. Is this true, Lila?"

"Mr. Capella, has had a lot of business clients out at the house. He likes to keep his business away from his family but any relationship with Mr. Dillinger is unknown to me. I did happen to meet him, though, Saul."

"Who, Lila?"

"John Dillinger... and do you know what the first thing he said to me, was? He took my hand and said, 'Hello, I rob banks for a living, what do you do?' Isn't that just a hoot?"

"Then, Mr. Dillinger has been at the house?"

"No! Of course not, Saul! I met Mr. Dillinger at a party in Chicago. He didn't stay very long, and I didn't see him leave-let me add that! "

"You've mentioned business associates are meeting at your home in Crystal Lake with Mr. Capella? I've heard that Capella is associating himself with some dangerous characters. By the way, why doesn't he carry on his business at his own home?"

"Mr. Capella likes to keep his family and business separate. I know his wife, Delores, just hates his business meetings! She's calling every ten seconds, never leaves him alone!"

"Well, Lila, she is his wife. You need to be very careful, sweetie. Please, I'm thinking of your safety, darling."

"I have nothing to be afraid of, Saul. Not the Germans, nor Delores, nor Mr. Capella's business associates."

"If you say so, darling. Just remember to heed my warn...oh, here's the countdown. Ten...nine...eight...seven...six...five...four...three...two...one...
Happy New Year, Lila and my listening friends!"

"Happy New Year, Saul!"

"...and a very Happy Birthday, Lila!"

"Thank you, darling Saul."

"This has been <u>An Evening in Chicago,</u> with me, your host, Saul Marvey. Good...Night!"

1936-New Year's Eve

There'll come a time when I'll be gone.
You'll never hear another song.
You'll never see me smile or cry
You'll just ask yourself, why?
All my troubles will fly away
And I'll find a brighter day...without you.

The love we shared will fade away
You'll have only my memory of yesterday.
When you think of me, please be kind
Remember all, I've left behind.
All my tears will be wiped dry
I'll no longer feel the need to cry...without you.

"Ladies and gentlemen, you have been listening to the late Lila Lane's latest release, "*Without You*" on WMAQ Radio's, An Evening in Chicago, with your host, Saul Marvey.

"Good evening, my listening friends. This is the eve of the New Year, 1936 and a lot has happened within the last few days of 1935.

Tonight, will be no celebration for me, but I will be remembering a dear, dear friend, Miss Lila Lane. For those of you who do not know of the tragedy that occurred only a day ago, I must inform you, and I apologize, before-hand, for any tears that I might shed. For you see, my dear listeners, yesterday morning, the body of Lila Lane, was found in her bedroom suite in Crystal Lake. She had been fatally shot and found lying, face down on her bed, by her personal assistant.

Excuse me...Ahem...Lila Lane was a very dear friend of mine. She was a regular New Year's Eve guest for the past eight years, never missed a year...ahem...until now. Who would do this terrible deed? Who would wipe out the life of such a lovely, wonderful woman? Lila would have been thirty-two, tomorrow. Just thirty-two! During the past eight New Year's Eves, Lila and I talked about a great many things; her movie and record career, her club, travel, associates and friends, and her home in Crystal Lake. She loved that home so much. She thought of it as a haven, and to think it became her place of death. Please excuse me, listeners. There'll be a little break and I'll be back."

We're back on the air, friends, and I have just been handed a breaking news report.

It reads: *The Chicago Police Department have announced a few persons of interest, in the Lila Lane Murder Case. They are questioning Mr. John Capella, Benny Chapman, well-known Mafia associate, and Wilhelm Heis, member of the Nazi Regime, who just so happens to be in Chicago this week. Stay tuned to WMAQ for the latest update on this case.*

That's the report, ladies and gentlemen and now the countdown to 1937.

Ten...nine...eight...you count for me, listeners. Happy New Year, friends and Happy Birthday, Lila. I will miss you, terribly. This has been An Evening in Chicago and I'm your host, Saul Marvey.
Good...Night!"

1976-December 30

"This is WMAQ Radio's Breaking News! It has just been reported that Mrs. Delores Capella, widow of the late Chicago Mob, John Capella, has just had Last Rites given to her and she has requested a meeting with Chicago's Police Commissioner and a Priest for Confession. More on this breaking story, as the facts are presented."

1976-New Year's Eve

"Breaking News from WMAQ! Delores Capella, at the age of eighty, has just been pronounced dead of natural causes. Before she succumbed, she held a meeting with the Police Commissioner where she reportedly confessed to the thirty-year-old murder of Lila Lane, singer and actress of the twenties and thirties. After confessing, Mrs. Capella peacefully passed away.

Miss Lane was shot once in the head at point blank range, in her home in Crystal Lake in 1936. It had once been thought that Miss Lane knew too much about Mr. Capella's enterprises which may had resulted in her murder and it was also reported at that time that Miss Lane was a spy, working for Jewish Intelligence, and was shot by a Nazi officer, Wilhelm Heis. However, Miss Lane's murder was never solved, and the case has remained open for thirty years.

Mrs. Capella confessed that she had knowledge of Miss Lane and Mr. Capella's affair for years and it got the best of her. Stealing a key, she found in her husband's pocket, Mrs. Capella took a gun and snuck into the Crystal Lake home, and quietly went up the back stairs and into Miss Lane's bedroom. Finding Miss Lane asleep, Mrs. Capella, placed the gun to the back of her head and fired one fatal shot. Mrs. Capella left as she had entered and then disposed of the gun by throwing it off of the Adams Street Bridge into the Chicago River. She then drove home and resumed her life.

What a tragic end to a wonderful entertainer and what a lifetime of guilt Delores Capella must have endured.

And now, WMAQ Radio presents, <u>An Evening in Chicago,</u> with your host, Saul Marvey Jr.

"The clouds have been broken.
The storm has ended.
The words were spoken.
My heart has been mended.

The sun is aglow; now.
The birds sing their song.
You finally know; how.
My life's moved along.

I promised you, I'd never have another.
You promised me, I'd always be your lover.
You promised to be – always there for me,
But that promised was shattered, somehow.

So, at last I am free from you now.

"You have just been listening to a recording of the late, Lila Lane. It was recorded late in 1935 and has only recently emerged on the music scene.

I'm Saul Marvey Jr. and I thank you for celebrating another New Year's Eve with us at WMAQ Radio's <u>An Evening in Chicago</u>.

We have a very special guest with us, tonight. Please Welcome, Chicago born, great-niece of Lila Lane, and recording star in her own right, Miss Liza Crane. We're so glad to have you with us. I've heard you've just bought your Aunt Lila's home in Crystal Lake. True? How is the new home?"

"In the words of my Aunt Lila: "*The house is peachy-keen,* Saul."

About the Author

Kathy grew up on Strasburg's Grasshopper Level and was a 1967 graduate of Pequea Valley High School.

She spent most of her young adult life as a fulltime mother to three daughters and was known as "mom" to all of the neighborhood children. A local Girl Scout leader, softball coach, and community theatre actress, in her spare time she was a painter and writer. Although she was never published professionally before her death, her stories and plays were enjoyed by many in Lancaster County, Pennsylvania and Nashville, Tennessee.

At the age of 40, she received her Bachelor of Science Degree in Elementary Education from Penn State Harrisburg, Summa Cum Laude. She was a science, social studies teacher and the director of the drama club at Bailey Middle School in Nashville, TN, until she retired in 2009.

Unfortunately, Kathy passed away from Lung Cancer in 2014 after a long hard-fought battle, but will always be loved and remembered. She dreamt of being published professionally and it is our sincerest honor to fulfill that dream.

Willow Moon Publishing

Wind and Water: A Love Story
The Little Dragon Flies in the Sun
Nobody Reads Haiku
Granny Kat's The Frog Prince (play adaptation)
Granny Kat's Sleeping Beauty (play adaptation)
S.H Levan's Cookbook: Recipes from Victorian Lancaster County
Pepper, Ms. Pepperoni, Finds Someone to Love

Coming Soon:
Samuel Stanley Scotty Snight by Alison Broderick
Make a Wish on a Fish by Jennie Wiley
The Itch of Gloria Fitch: a play by Paul Hood
Sweet Treats Book of Cupcakes: A Love You a Brunch Cookbook edited by M. L. Ashly

https://willowmoonpub.com